# MAVERICK MARSHAL

When Ben Galliard sets out in Montana to seek his brother Frank, he clashes with a band of rustlers led by the ruthless McCabe. Recovering from this ordeal he meets an attractive young woman, Colly Wells, who is also seeking Frank, claiming that he has killed her grandpa.

Events lead Ben into a gunfight at the throwback town of Bleak Springs, after which he is elected marshal and faces the additional challenge of thwarting McCabe's plans. The quest takes him to the thriving town of Sparville, where he contends with more discords between Colly and Frank, and confronts an unhelpful sheriff who stifles his efforts to tackle McCabe. But will he survive the double showdown to come?

# MAVERICK MARSHAL

HARLAN KENT

ROBERT HALE · LONDON

© Harlan Kent 1991
First published in Great Britain 1991

ISBN 0 7090 4614 6

Robert Hale Limited
Clerkenwell House
Clerkenwell Green
London EC1R 0HT

The right of Harlan Kent to be identified as
author of this work has been asserted by him
in accordance with the Copyright, Designs and
Patents Act 1988.

Photoset in North Wales by
Derek Doyle & Associates, Mold, Clwyd.
Printed and bound in Great Britain by WBC Print Ltd,
and WBC Bookbinders Ltd, Bridgend, Glamorgan.

# ONE

Ben Galliard came across the dead horse when he was a day's ride west of the Rocking Y. He swung from his roan stallion and rested a hand on the carcass. It was still warm. A foreleg was broken and someone had put a bullet through the critter's brain before stripping off the saddle.

From beneath the brim of his Montana peak hat, Ben scanned the uneventful landscape. He studied the buffalo grass, still sodden from the winter thaws. His sign-reading was skilled enough to make intelligent guesses.

A number of cattle and horses had passed, maybe an hour previously. Other footprints were man-made and there had been considerable trampling.

The reason seemed clear. Some riders had been helping one of their party whose mount had come to grief. Ben's keen eye picked out blood splashes in the mud. Someone had suffered.

He remounted. Glancing ahead, he wondered why such a small herd had been driven towards the Montana foothills. Any Rocking Y strays should have been headed back towards the spread for round-up. He also recalled rumours of rustling. According to Harvey Jensen, the tough fair-minded owner of the Rocking Y, some of the smaller outfits could be running low on scruples.

Ben nudged his horse forward until he came to a

shallow stream – a meltwater run-off that would eventually drain into a tributary of the Musselshell. Cattle and riders had continued upstream. Standing in the stirrups Ben spotted a dark hump on the ground ahead. He urged the roan into a trot. As he came up with caution, the prone man made no movement.

Ben dismounted for a closer look. If this was the rider of the dead horse the saddle was still missing. He was a weedy, undernourished hombre, or had been. There was a bullet hole next to his spine and he had been left to rot.

Straightening up with a nudge of distaste, Ben wondered whether to tackle a burial but was short of shovelling gear. Then a wispy smudge against the hills caught his eye.

He reached for his saddlepouch and lugged out his field glasses – a Civil War relic from his Uncle Denzil some five years back. These revealed a thin curl of smoke rising from beyond a ridge into the afternoon sky. Maybe someone warming his toes by a campfire had some explaining to do.

A dead horse; a dead man ... Ben set off towards the smoke.

And ran into trouble.

The stream emerged from a delve in the foothills. The dispersing smoke suggested that the fire was low down in a depression. Ben cut round to higher ground where his approach might be less obvious. Soon he was gazing down upon a branding party on the flat floor of a secluded hollow. Opposite him, the stream dribbled down the steep northern face. It ran out southwards along a short canyon.

The fire was smouldering amid a scattering of rocks. Three rough-cut men were tackling a roped calf with a hot iron. A fourth, in a coonskin cap, was sitting by the stream, showing no interest.

Towards the back of the hollow some forty head of restless longhorns, including several calves, were clustered in a makeshift corral of strung ropes. They were being watched by a lean individual on a yellow-flanked claybank.

Ben studied the scene through his glasses. He counted two more men loafing beyond the cattle, then an eighth sitting on a rock up the rear face with a rifle straddling his knees. A lookout. He did not appear to be taking his job seriously.

Ben viewed the beeves again. Here and there he picked out a Rocking Y brand, but most of the calves appeared unmarked. None of these men were Rocking Y hands, and Ben had been waddying that spread close on ten months. He lowered the glasses, resting them against the pommel. His eyes glinted, shrewd and blue, in features honed by work and weather. Texas-bred, going on thirty, his slim agile build cut a stark figure in the saddle.

This was really none of his concern. He had ceased to act for Mr Jensen. But he still felt kind of indebted.

Two sundowns ago Jensen had hinted he would be short-handed. The foreman, Dan Fallows, had ridden over to Bleak Springs hoping to find more men, leaving Ben to face Jensen.

'I can't persuade you?' Jensen had made a last attempt. 'With the oncoming season I'll need all the riders I can get.'

Ben shook his head. 'Thanks, Mr Jensen. But I still got that unfinished business to take care of.'

'Looking for that brother of yours? I thought you'd given that up. My foreman reckoned you were settled here.'

'I was, almost. When I joined you after last year's drive, I was hoping Frank might be waddying around these parts. He'd come up the same trail the previous year.'

'Maybe, but surely Fallows confirmed that Frank Galliard never took on as a hand. Why pull out now?'

'One of the men remembered Frank; reckoned he might have headed for the mining camps above Sparville.'

'Seeking gold?' Jensen released a sigh of disappointment. 'He'd do better bounty-hunting for prairie wolves.' He began to count from a roll of greenbacks. 'Here's your dues. But don't expect a grub stake.'

'It's a family matter.' Ben stuffed the bills away. 'After Pa died, Ma wanted me to find Frank to handle the ranch. I'm not surprised if he's lit out for the camps. Pa's brother Denzil went prospecting at Sparville after the War. If it suits, I'll leave in the morning.'

So Ben had collected his bedroll and rain slicker from the bunkhouse, cleaned his Colt .45 and Springfield carbine, and ridden out under the gunmetal light of yesterday's dawn.

As he sat now astride the roan, his attention was divided between the fire below and questioning his own wisdom. He watched a curl of smoke rise as the hot iron was applied to the calf's coat, but it was difficult to discern the brand.

He was about to seek a closer look when a hoof-fall from behind was followed by the unmistakable click of a weapon. He tensed back on the cantle, right hand dropping towards the butt of the Colt resting against his hip.

'Keep 'em high, stranger,' a gritty voice said.

Scolding his lapse of attention, Ben kept both hands in view, left one gripping the glasses. He assessed his challenger who was advancing on a piebald, clutching a Winchester carbine. Ben looked into corrosive eyes shaded by a greasy hat brim.

'Where you heading?' The man spoke through taut lips.

'West Montana,' Ben answered in an easy voice.

'What's concernin' you here?'

'I could ask you the same question.'

'Don't get skittish with me, mister.' The stubbly jaw began to baccy-chew as the man considered his next move.

A voice from the hollow called up: 'Nat, bring him in.'

'You hear that? Suppose we go talk with McCabe?'

'Is he your ramrod? I was just gonna pay my respects.'

As Ben reached to secure the glasses the grip on the carbine stiffened. 'And keep your hands out of them pouches. Move.'

Ben shrugged laconically. This hombre looked edgy enough to shoot. With controlled movements Ben looped the neckstrap of the glasses over his saddle horn and set the roan to pick a downslope route. The other rider followed until they crossed the stream to where the men were grouped.

Ben caught the strong waft of burnt hair and hide. The three men with the calf watched his arrival.

'Leave him to me, Nat.' The lean man kneed his claybank forward. He looked suave, collected. The hair spilling from under his hat was as fair as straw. He was carrying a quirt and he confronted Ben with chill slate eyes.

'Howdy.' Ben broke the silence with a congenial nod. 'Been gathering yourselves a bunch of strays?'

The man ignored the question. 'What outfit you from?' His voice was husky, lined with menace.

'No outfit. I'm heading for west Montana.'

The branders had drawn forward. One of them continued coiling up a grass rope. The lookout on the rock face had made no move. Nor had the man languishing by the stream; his coonskin was askew to reveal a bloodstained bandana wrapped around his head.

Ben glanced at the calf renewing acquaintance with the mother cow. He took in the smouldering iron clutched by a blotchy-faced hunk of saddle fat in a java shirt and plainsman hat.

'That sure looks like a Cut Circle iron you're holding.'

The lean rider nudged his claybank closer to Ben. His voice softened to a near-whisper. 'If you're heading west, I'd do so while you're still able.'

Ben nodded, contemplating. 'Might at that. But it ain't difficult to smother a Rocking Y brand with a Cut Circle iron. And as for Cut Circle calves making up to Rocking Y mothers ...'

Nat chipped in, scratching at his stubble. 'He'd been up on the rim a good coupla minutes, McCabe. Spying on us.'

'Spying with those?' McCabe jabbed the handle of his quirt at the glasses dangling from Ben's saddle horn.

Suppressing a tingle of anger, Ben steadied the roan. 'Why not? Someone's been hazing off the stock around these parts.'

'And who did you haze these off?' McCabe poked the quirt through the strap of the glasses. 'A dead general?'

Ben sucked in a breath. 'If you're gonna talk about dead men, there's one on the range with a hole in his back.'

McCabe prickled, then released a strident laugh. 'Is that what's eating you? A couple of hours, and we'll be gone.'

The man in the coonskin and bloodstained bandana gave a phlegmatic cough. 'Hey, McCabe,' he called across in some distress. 'I thought we was holing up here till dark.'

'Calm down, Clipper. Give that sore brain a rest.'

Clipper grumbled, 'Ain't my fault, hoss bustin' a leg.'

If Clipper had been on the dead horse, Ben guessed, he could have hit his head in the tumble. And Ben reckoned this hollow was too disorganised for an overnight camp. Perhaps McCabe had only halted for Clipper to drag himself together; none of the mounts had been off-saddled. Then the branding trio had begun to fill in time.

McCabe was still watching Ben with those chilly eyes.

'We've got more at stake than branding a few beeves. You say you ain't with any outfit? You could even ride with us –'

He broke off as Clipper began to cough afresh. The man with the grass rope, a stocky hombre in a smoky grey jacket and weathered stetson, called out: 'Clipper, we should have dropped you back there too, nursing a slug like your hoss.'

'Very funny.' Clipper gave a surly growl, and spat.

McCabe addressed the stocky man: 'Chub, watch your tongue.' To Clipper, he said: 'If you don't piece yourself together, you get left. This drifter ain't taking up my offer, so why not try his roan? Fine horseflesh; good Texas saddle. Better than that nag you finished up on –'

'This roan already has a rider,' Ben snapped. He guessed there must have been a squabble when they lost a horse. 'So who owned Clipper's nag? The dead hombre?'

At this second mention of the shot man, McCabe smiled, unperturbed. 'We decided to dispense with him.'

Clipper roused a protest: 'Weren't my doing, that.'

'So whose was it?' Ben met McCabe's ice-chip eyes.

With a sudden twitch of the quirt handle, McCabe flipped the strap of the glasses from Ben's saddle horn.

Ben was ready. As he grabbed the whip and yanked it towards him he glimpsed Nat taking a snap aim. McCabe bumped against Ben; their horses wheeled. Grabbing McCabe's coat, Ben wrenched him closer as Nat's carbine crashed. He felt the breeze of a bullet, but it skimmed high in order to miss McCabe.

Ben jerked out his scroll-engraved Colt. It glinted as it roared. Nat howled as the carbine went pitching from his torn knuckles. Slithering, Ben kicked free of the stirrups and landed in a crouch. McCabe swung himself straight in the saddle.

The others were slow to react. Chub and the third brander, a bearded rough in a fancy tan stetson, scampered for their horses. Swinging his rope, Chub vaulted on to a dappled grey; the other snatched a Winchester from his sorrel and loosed off a round, wild enough to miss. As it creased the rump of McCabe's claybank Ben dropped the bearded man with a single shot.

McCabe grappled for his Colt. As the claybank shied Ben glimpsed the cutaway trigger-guard. McCabe's shot veered, peeling Ben's left sleeve and forearm. Before he could wince, a spinning loop fell around his chest. Chub spurred the grey. The loop tightened and Ben hit the ground.

He heard a harsh laugh, saw McCabe taking leisurely aim; then a surging amid the cattle caught the rustler's attention.

'Hold your fire,' McCabe yelled.

Chub was cantering his grey towards the stream.

Ben bumped over rocks, clawing at the pinioning rope; he knew the danger from a spooked herd in a confined space. McCabe seemed torn between calming the beeves and relishing the entertainment.

The grey splashed into the shallows, dragging Ben after it. He stemmed a torrent of abuse as his revolver jerked free into the water. He tried to jam his heels into the streambed and the rowels of his spurs grated over stones.

Chub circuited back; the rope slackened. Squirming on to one knee, Ben worked an arm free. Then the rope toppled him again. With his advantage lost he found himself slithering up the muddy bank as Chub beelined for the fire.

The core was red under a shroud of ash. Ben churned through it amid sparks and acrid fumes. Embers scorched his wrist and he cursed his lack of gauntlets. He cursed Chub's ancestry, but his words were a choking cough. Only his soaked clothing gave some measure of protection.

McCabe chortled. 'Take the bastard round again. This time leave him to fry.'

Ben slid towards the stream as Chub began a second lap. If he could slice the rope with his Bowie ... He picked out Nat, white-faced and nursing his hand. And Clipper, watching vacantly. And the blotchy brander, stooping over the bearded rough alongside the sorrel.

'Hey, McCabe,' Blotchy called. 'Renny ain't so good. He's stopped one in the chest.'

'Shit.' McCabe holstered his Colt. 'We need Renny –'

Ben hit the stream, swallowing water. Sight and sound became a blur. Then the rope was heaving him like a sodden log back towards the fire.

Ben retched. His eyes opened to imbibe the rockface where the lookout sat high and aloof, viewing the combat like a rodeo spectator.

Three yards from the fire, Ben rammed his heels against the windbreak rocks. Chub checked and wheeled the grey, trying to swing the rope high across the embers. As the dally loosened on the saddle horn, Ben seized his slender chance. Smoke swirled to mask his movement as he yanked at the stop-knot. The loop slipped down over his body.

Grabbing the cool end of a half-burned faggot, Ben hurled it. Chub ducked his head. The faggot soared past him into the milling longhorns, scattering sparks off a startled bull.

As Ben kicked free of the loop, the cable corral broke. He hurled a second firebrand straight at the beeves.

'Watch the herd,' McCabe bawled. To Chub, he snarled: 'I thought you'd got the sonofabitch roped ...' And a mass of longhorn flesh burst forth.

Ben stumbled aside, flinching from abrasions and burns. Close by, near a panicky skewbald, someone's carbine rested on a boulder. Ben dived for it but tripped and sprawled, failing to snatch it.

Just then the lookout chose to act. His rifle echoed off the rear rockface. Pebbles spurted up against Ben's nose. He lay motionless, shamming dead. The beeves plunged down-canyon for open country.

'Head 'em off!' As McCabe slewed the claybank he loosed a parting shot at Ben, misjudging his target.

With one ear pressed on a stone, Ben listened to the magnified thunder of receding hooves. Through slitted eyes he saw Blotchy looming up. The brander rammed the iron into its sheath on the skewbald, thrust the carbine into his saddle boot, swung into leather and was away.

The lookout came skittering down the rockface with sliding footholds. He jumped astride a paint which he thrashed into a departing gallop.

As the turmoil faded, Ben eased himself up. He saw his roan, frisking downstream, and gave his two-note whistle to calm it. They respected each other. Unlike men.

And two wounded men still remained.

Ben tried a shaky step or two, limping from a bruised knee. His scorched, wet clothing hindered him. He glanced at Clipper who had not shifted and was staring at him sullenly. Renny, the other wounded rustler, lay semi-conscious.

Ben picked up his hat and slapped off the mud. He rescued his revolver from the stream and found his field glasses. One lens was splintered; the other side still worked. From the items scattered around, he guessed the rustlers would soon be back.

Clipper watched fearfully as Ben gave a cursory check on his water-sodden Colt. 'You gonna use that thing?' His speech sounded slurred, almost incoherent.

'I sure ain't aimin' to sling it away.' Ben took the revolvers from Clipper's and Renny's gunbelts, collected Nat's carbine and Renny's Winchester, and chucked the lot into the stream. 'You and your hoss got me into this, you know that?'

'I didn't invite you. I got no quarrel with you, mister.'

'So how come you're mixing with McCabe?'

'Drifted in. McCabe's building up a band.'

'For running off beeves? I counted nine men all told.'

'Not for rustling. He's due to meet some others.'

'What for?' Ben caught the reins on the roan. 'Where at?'

'Blackfoot Bluff. We ain't all cowpokes. Me, I was weaned on sheep.' To Ben, reared on cow, the thought of sheep set his stomach curdling. 'I'll tell you this much, mister. You ain't chosen easy, tangling with McCabe.'

'It was his choice.' Stiffly, Ben began to mount up. 'What's keeping you anyway, if you ain't taken with him?'

Clipper gazed mournfully at his wounded companion. 'Me and Renny's been sticking together. McCabe wants him for something.'

'Renny don't look like he's shifting far. Nor do you. What happened to your head?'

Clipper touched the bloodsoaked bandana. 'Hoss threw me. I got Renny to thank for helping me. I could have been left lying out there like that saddlebum Hank Willis.'

'The one shot in the back?'

Clipper's voice grew slurred. 'He tried to argue too big a party could reduce everyone's cut of the share-out.'

'Share-out of what?'

Clipper seemed not to hear. 'So McCabe gave Willis his comeuppance.' He gave an exhausted cough.

'Where's McCabe taking those beeves? Cut Circle?' When Clipper didn't reply, Ben said: 'You'd better haul yourself over and look at Renny. He needs some attention.'

As Ben wheeled the roan and urged it out of the hollow he was counting the scores he had to settle with McCabe.

# TWO

Ben paused on higher ground to view the rustlers through the intact half of his glasses. They were pinpoints of movement, working ahead of the herd. He managed a grim smile. Surprising, the chaos a small stampede could create. He descended to flatter terrain, hoping the cattle, would keep McCabe occupied.

He freshened up at a waterhole, but preferred to seek a stream before topping up his canteen. His abrasions were more sore than severe. He massaged his knee, wondering whether to don woollens, but he was already drying out and feeling more comfortable. 'You got a durned lucky streak, Ben Galliard,' he muttered to himself.

He cleaned his Colt and clipped dry shells into his gunbelt. He remounted and held the roan at a trot to the north-west. There was no recognisable trail until he neared Buffalo Skulls where animal bones marked a desolate fork in the east-west stage road from Bleak Springs to Sparville City. The northern branch led back towards Bleak. A sign painted on a rock by the southern leg said: *ROCKING Y – 45 MILES*.

Ben crossed the road and cut up into the timber. Both routes led to Sparville but the hills gave better promise of streams.

Close on sundown he found his stream with a pleasant dell near its bank. Before off-saddling he gathered brushwood and lit himself a fire. As the flames took he began to reflect.

He expected the rustlers to continue south-west. Blackfoot Bluff lay that way; so did the Cut Circle spread. It was unlikely he would cross trails again with McCabe just yet. When he had reached Sparville in two days time he hoped to concentrate on seeking Frank out in the mining camps.

Watching the incandescence creeping up the twigs, Ben wondered if he was doing the sensiblest thing. Should he be returning to inform Mr Jensen about the rustling? Charlie Priest, the town marshal at Bleak Springs, was supposed to be dealing with it; but it would not surprise Ben if Jensen preferred to roust up some trustworthy riders to settle matters himself. But Ben did not want to be deflected from his search for Frank.

Four years back, Uncle Denzil's last letter to Pa had come from Sparville. Denzil was hoping his claim would strike lucky, but no one even knew if he was still alive. Maybe Frank was hoping to find both Uncle Denzil *and* gold.

If he couldn't locate Frank – what then? Ben didn't fancy months of trying to wash nuggets from a stream. It hadn't needed Jensen to tell him that hitting pay-dirt was chancy.

But those rustlers disturbed him. Except for maybe McCabe and Chub, they lacked experience in punching. They were more like baptised gunfighters. Renny hardly had the calloused hands of a cattleworker. And what was Clipper, a sheepman, doing among them? Genuine cowmen would never have accepted him.

With mixed feelings, Ben fanned the flames with his hat. A sneaky recognition told him he should not condemn Clipper for rearing woollybacks. It made more sense to blacklist him for riding with McCabe.

Ben emptied a can of sausages into his skillet and began to cook. He was about to leave them frizzling while he unsaddled the roan when a gunshot rang out from beyond a nearby rise.

Ben set the skillet down. He stood up, buckling on his gunbelt. He could see no one about; but after today he preferred to know who was shooting at what, even if it turned out to be some old sourdough picking off a jack-rabbit supper.

Peering out of the dell he saw a riderless horse galloping into the middle distance. Ignoring the waft of cooking sausages Ben mounted his roan and emerged from the dell, keeping his eyes skinned. The horse had halted a half mile away and seemed at peace with itself. Ben veered aside, picking a path through scrub and rock. In the declining light he saw nothing significant. No one betrayed a presence, yet he felt he was being watched. He circuited round towards the runaway.

It was a black mare, trailing a rein. Empty rifle scabbard, good quality saddle; full-looking pouches. The mare gave a toss of the head and did not object when Ben caught its rein.

'Easy girl,' he soothed. 'Let's go find your rider.'

Leading the runaway, Ben detoured back past some deadfall timber. He was about to quit the search and take the mare along to his fire when a voice called: 'Hold it, mister.'

Ben froze. The voice was a woman's. His eyes scanned the shadows for detail. He spotted a rifle barrel resting in a crevice and the black brim of a hat, but the face stayed hidden.

'Drop the reins on that mare, then back off.'

Ben managed a cautious smile. 'Yours, is she?' He did as asked, allowing the mare to amble, and sat with his arms uplifted. 'I thought someone had me bushwhacked.'

'You still could be. Now, back off!' The snap in her voice made him appreciate the tautness of her nerves.

Ben glanced around the rocks again. 'Look, lady – I take take it you're alone. So what spooked your mare?' He tried an inviting chuckle. 'I'd come out before she blocks your aim.'

The woman hesitated. 'First I want to know who you are and where you're headin'.'

'I don't see how that helps, but the name's Ben. Yesterday I quit the Rocking Y. I'm heading for a half-cooked supper half a mile west. Making coffee, if you feel like trying some.'

The woman edged from the rock, still keeping a tight bead on Ben. She was darkish with a dusky skin, almost gold-tinted by the setting sun. She wore a flat-crowned hat, slim black riding boots and a thick buckskin coat that almost hid her checkered shirt and cream bandana. Her split tan skirt was designed for warmth and swung attractively as she stepped further out.

'What did I ever do against you?' asked Ben.

'I don't trust a man till he's accounted for himself.'

'I just did. You're mighty suspicious.' Ben held his encouraging smile. 'Not that I blame you for playing safe.'

'I'm a great believer in self-protection.'

'Protection from what?'

She wavered, then relaxed her grip on the rifle. 'Take a look beyond that stretch of grass.'

Hoping this was not some trick, Ben obliged. The motionless head and claws of a large cat projected from the scrub.

'You killed yourself a mountain lion?' he said in wonder.

'It sprang from those rocks.' She gave a shudder. 'The mare threw me. I managed to grab the rifle as she took off.'

Enlightened Ben dismounted for a closer inspection.

'I was lucky, I guess.' The girl faltered, clearly shaken.

'Yeah.' Ben toed the dead catamount. 'As long as you ain't aimin' to give me the same treatment,' he drawled, and saw a smile twitch at her lips; but she remained wary of him. 'If you're interested in that coffee, it's just over that rise.' He swung back into leather. 'Come along before it's dark.'

In the cluttered camp at Blackfoot Bluff, Clipper hunched over the fire and pulled the poncho tighter round his shoulders. He felt miserable, confused. And his head kept hurting.

But for McCabe's rustling spree none of this would have happened. Crazy venture. Clipper touched the congealed blood on his bandana bandage. He knew he wasn't right. He could remember the stranger, the guntalk, the stampede ... By the time McCabe had rounded up the cattle the stranger was clean away.

'Gather the gear,' McCabe had ordered on returning to the hollow. 'That sonofabitch could be back with extras.'

They had trussed Clipper to his saddle horn to prop him upright, but draping Renny on a hoss had posed problems.

Chub snorted. 'Renny'll be a gonner soon.'

'Just stanch his bleeding and get him to Blackfoot Bluff,' McCabe snapped. 'Then we can rig him a bed on the wagon.'

They'd brought the wagon along four days back. From Bleak Springs, when McCabe started to assemble his band. Befuddled, Clipper wondered now how he had survived the recent ride here. Even moreso, how Renny had endured the jolting.

An aroma of coffee set Clipper's juices astir. He

counted himself lucky. McCabe could have left him stranded but he needed him to care for Renny. Maybe that was what kept Clipper going. McCabe was targeting for the big money, so whatever it was he wanted from Renny had to be important.

Clipper gazed mournfully into the flames. Was no one bringing him coffee? The tang faded, leaving only the smoky reek of the fire. They were neglecting him again.

For most of his life he'd been despised by cattlemen. It was no different riding with this rabble. That was why they called him Clipper – the sheep-shearing sonofabitch. Only Renny treated him with any respect.

And Renny looked to be dying.

Ben was adding kindling to his fire when the girl rode in. She dismounted with easy grace, leaving her rifle in its scabbard as she brought a mug from her saddle pouch.

Ben glanced at her. 'Sausages got kinda charred, and water ain't boiling yet.'

She knelt by the flames, keeping her distance from him.

'Gets chilly these evenings,' he remarked. 'You got a plate? If you want some hot dogs you're gonna need one.'

'Sure I got a plate. You think I was brought up eating from the skillet?' She cast a doubtful eye over his meal. 'You ain't got many sausages. I could do us some flapjacks.'

'A two-course dinner? Suits me.'

As the young woman prepared flapjacks she stayed immersed in her thoughts. Ben watched her covertly, wondering if she was in some trouble. When they had eaten and were sipping coffee, she relaxed a little. She drew closer to the fire, hugging her arms round her knees.

'Thanks anyway, mister,' she said.

'Ben,' he reminded her. 'For what? Sharing a meal?'

'For recovering Belle – my mare.'

He shrugged. 'Weren't nothing.' He threw on another faggot. 'You got a name too?'

'Sure I got a name.' She threw him a look as though he had asked a stupid question. 'It's Cornelia Wells. Folk back home usually call me Colly.'

'And which way's home?'

She gave a reticent sigh. 'Pa took a homestead twenty miles east of Bleak Springs. I just tried being a laundress in Sparville, but it weren't for me.'

'I hear Sparville's a big town.'

'Sure. It's civilized. Ain't you bin there?'

'I'm heading that way, for the mining camps.'

She weighed him with eyes of liquid sienna, her hair clustering her shoulders in dark alluring curls. 'You don't look like a prospector. No pack mule?'

'I was a ranch hand till night before last.'

'At the Rocking Y?' She peered closer. 'What happened to your face? You're all bruised. Your shirt's all scorched.'

Ben raised a short laugh. 'I ran into some jaspers who were working the brands.' He explained briefly his ordeal. 'They most likely headed south-west to Blackfoot Bluff.'

'I know it. So what's the attraction of the mining camps?'

Ben hesitated. 'I'm seeking my eldest brother, Frank. He could be there.' He shifted his sore limbs. 'What lured you to Sparville, Colly? Surely not laundry work.'

She made a sad ruck with her lips. 'Grandpa was prospecting there; I went to visit him. He lived in a log-cabin near the timber. He reckoned he'd never struck rich, though some said he'd hit pay-dirt months back and was waiting for the thaws to visit the assay office. A six-hour trip through snow. But there was some shotgun trouble. Now, Grandpa's dead.'

'You mean someone cut him down? Do they know who?'

'Oh, sure. Some drifter he'd befriended. Name of Galliard.'

Ben Galliard went still for a moment, then began to swill coffee dregs from his mug.

'Was this man arrested?'

'Yeah, by Sheriff Quayle. But he broke jail. Quayle was livid. Galliard could have headed for Bleak Springs.'

'How d'you know that?'

'A shrewd guess. He'd been a cattleworker once and reckoned the Rocking Y could be a good spread to work for.' She glanced at Ben. 'You never came across a Galliard, did you, while you were at the Rocking Y? It ain't a common handle.'

Ben set his mug aside. 'Can't say I met him there,' he answered truthfully. 'You know his first name?'

'No, oddly enough. The sheriff just called him Galliard. Grandpa no doubt knew, but usually referred to him as Gal.'

Ben eased a breath of relief, glad he had not revealed his own second name. But what could Frank have got mixed up in?

'So are you ridin' back to the homestead now?'

'Sure. I got to let my folks know Grandpa's dead.'

'You ain't taking it on yourself to chase this Galliard?'

'Sure I'm chasing him,' she said in deadly earnest. 'He blasted Grandpa with a load of buckshot. If I find him, maybe I'll haul him back to Sparville at gunpoint.'

'Colly, it may not be safe going hell-bent alone after Galliard. Isn't Sheriff Quayle doing anything about it?'

'Quayle won't drag his butt outside of Sparville.'

'Then why not talk to the Bleak Springs marshal?'

'Charlie Priest?' Colly looked dubious. 'I bin told not to put much faith in him.'

'Yeah, well ...' Ben released a cynical smirk. 'It's true he ain't what he was. Jensen, the Rocking Y boss, has been on at him for months.' He paused. 'Was Quayle sure he'd got the right man?'

'Why shouldn't he be? There was a witness – Hayley. He saw Galliard taking a shotgun into Grandpa's cabin. What's more, an uncle of Galliard's, name of Denzil, had been Grandpa's pard. Denzil died two years back. Pneumonia. But his gold was missing. Quayle thinks Grandpa took it. But there was no gold found in the cabin. Quayle reckons Galliard stole it back.'

'D'you believe your Grandpa took Denzil's gold?'

'Not a chance.' Colly shook her head. 'I'm not having his name slurred on top of him being shot.'

Ben pondered. This was a surprise, her Grandpa and Denzil being pards. Things may not sound rosy for Frank, but other facts were showing face. So Denzil had been dead two years ...

Ben wiped off his plate with a wad of clean grass. 'What does Galliard look like?' he asked.

'Tall, swarthy. Has a small scar by his left sideburn. I've seen him a time or two. I'll know him again.'

Ben said nothing. He recalled Frank gashing his cheek in some kids' game. The flesh had taken time to heal.

Had he and Frank passed each other somewhere? He would like to hear his brother's version of the girl's story – preferably before she caught up with him. If he went back to the Rocking Y he might find Frank there already. But he only had Colly's say-so to go on.

'You look lost in thought,' Colly observed.

He blinked, feeling a touch of guilt. 'Just re-livin' that frying I took today. Right now I'm wondering if I did right to leave Jensen's spread.'

'So what's your next move?'

'I'm gonna sleep on it … You'd best put your bedroll by this fire. We could take turns on watch.'

'For mountain cats or rustlers?'

'Cats. I'm hoping I'm well clear of rustlers.'

She off-saddled the mare and arranged her blankets. As Ben laid his gunbelt handy he noticed her slipping a small handgun into her bedding.

'I hope that Derringer ain't hair-trigger, or you'll be shooting yourself in your sleep.'

'You weren't meant to see.' She gave an apologetic glance.

'I saw. You don't have to hide it on my account; I got no designs.' In the flickering fireglow, he could imagine she blushed. 'You wanna take first watch or second?'

'First,' she said. 'I ain't as bushed as you.'

On that he did not argue. Turning his back, he tugged the blankets to his chin. Colly sat watching images in the embers.

'Ben,' she asked presently, 'were you trying to convince yourself – that you should head back for the Rocking Y?'

'Why? You ain't fishing for company towards Bleak in case you collide with more mountain cats?'

'Look, mister' – her voice rose – 'I didn't do so damn bad on my own with that last one.'

Ben smiled behind closed eyelids, approving her spirit. 'I might consider escorting you,' he murmured, 'but you'll have to promise not to blow my head off.'

And beneath his smile, the true reason nagged.
He must find Frank before Colly did.

'Clipper!'

The sheepman jolted awake to find McCabe and two hard-bitten newcomers peering down at him – Pierre, a gingery French-Canadian; and Lou, a bulky gunhawk from Nebraska.

'You still got a sore head?' From McCabe, this sounded like an order. 'Lou and Pierre are going to fetch Doc Mason from Bleak Springs to look at Renny. You're going with them.'

'To Bleak?' Clipper floundered, blinking in the firelight.

'Bleak ain't far. You can ride, can't you?'

Clipper didn't answer. 'You gonna move the beeves?'

'Forget the beeves. They're gone.'

He raked through confused impressions that had assailed him during his dozing: men arriving, money changing hands.

'Can't you send Renny into Bleak?' he asked hazily.

'Renny's in bad shape; we need him conscious. Get that skull seen to and I'll have more faith in you. It's good credential. Could help persuade Mason to come out without being leant on. We don't have to tell him Renny's harbouring a slug till he gets here.'

'What if I hold things up?'

'Then Lou and Pierre might drop you as coyote meat.'

Clipper shifted his limbs. He wished he knew more. All McCabe had promised were big profits. Ample men, a large take, a worthwhile share-out. Same as in his earlier robberies.

McCabe addressed Lou. 'We've a day or two to kill before Slim Cricklewood arrives, then I still gotta convince him of the change of plan. But that's no excuse for dawdling.'

'We'll see to it,' said Lou.

Feeding Clipper a cold-steel stare, McCabe added: 'And stay on your hoss. When you get back you can nurse Renny like he was one of your precious woollybacks.' He turned away.

Pierre said curtly: 'Be ready to ride in five minutes.'

Head throbbing, Clipper struggled free of the blankets.

# THREE

Colly roused Ben after first watch then snuggled into her bedroll. Ben sat out the uneventful hours. By dawn he knew what he must do.

He fuelled the dying campfire, made coffee, then wakened Colly with a steaming mug. 'Early breakfast,' he said.

She stirred reluctantly. 'My thanks.' She took a sip.

When they had eaten, he sorted out his pouches. 'I'll accompany you as far as Buffalo Skulls, then I'm taking the south fork. You can head on into Bleak. I want to tell Jensen about the rustling.' And, he hoped, maybe run into Frank as a bonus.

Colly looked him over, the strengthening light kissing a gloss into her hair. 'You could do with visiting Bleak yourself to buy a new coat and shirt. They still sell 'em. Place did a fair trade when it grew up fifteen years back.'

'Yeah, until the big strikes occurred at Sparville; then Bleak died a death. Fool's gold and false promise.'

Yet it had survived. Jensen represented the ranchers on its council. Supplies passed through. The stage banked money into Sparville and shipped assayed gold east.

'You bin to Bleak Springs much?' Colly asked.

'A time or two. And you?'

'A time or two. My folk saw it when they first

came westering. It was losing popularity even then.'

But it had clung to its name from the same stubborn pride by which it kept its ageing marshal, Charlie Priest.

Ben doused the fire and they struck camp. As they talked along the east-going trail Ben was encouraged to note her strengthening confidence in him.

'Do your folk scrape enough to live on as nesters?'

'Yeah.' She glanced at him. 'Anything wrong with that?'

'No, I guess not.' Ben tried to hide his disapproval. 'Just that nesters and stockbreeders don't always mix.'

'So? There's room for everyone, mister.'

Ben dropped the tender topic. His leaning was towards the ranchers; but sometimes he felt he did not try enough to see the homesteader's point of view.

In a while she asked: 'You bin with cattle all your life?'

He grinned, reminiscing. 'I been misfit at a few things. Even studied law. Still got a textbook in my saddle pouch.'

'Guess I bin a misfit too. As a girl, I wanted to act. I was always reading plays. But Pa didn't hold with it.'

'You'd have made a fine actress. You're clean-cut, pretty enough.' Ben glimpsed her modest smile. 'Now me, I came up from Texas after my Pa died. That's why I'm seeking my brother. Pa had ruled it's up to Frank to run the ranch.' He hesitated. 'If you don't find this Galliard, do you keep going east?'

'Guess so. The folk got to be told about Grandpa.'

Ben let it rest there. He didn't want her thinking he had some special interest in the Galliard man.

They passed no one. The air smelt crisp, and further south the land was greening up with rich pasture. Towards noon they reached the stage road and began to pick out bleached bones.

'Buffalo Skulls,' Ben said. 'Here's where I cut off, Colly. When you get to Bleak Springs have a word with the marshal. He ought to know who's turned up in town.'

Colly smiled goodbye. 'Hope you find your brother. Will you be in Bleak these next few days?'

'Can't rightly say. Depends on Jensen.'

Ben touched his hat in laconic farewell as she spurred the mare away. He watched her receding down the road and felt tainted with his own deceit.

As the roan clopped along, Ben took time pondering on whether his advice to Colly over Frank was unfair. Even if she contacted the Bleak Springs marshal he would most likely shrug his shoulders to Sparville trouble. Charlie Priest, like Sheriff Quayle apparently, preferred to sit on his butt.

Priest always claimed he had enough to handle in Bleak. Snag was, he handled little. He seldom rode far since a wiry stallion had injured his leg. Some said he had been appointed from outside – a showpiece to give the town status. No younger peace officer willing to serve had been found. Several years on, Priest was still wearing his star and presiding with sleepy contentment.

His hoosegow was seldom used, apart from cooling off the odd roistering cowboy. Come round-up time, Jensen had rules on that: 'Any hand of mine must be fit from Day One, not in jug sleeping off rotgut.'

Ben had occasionally drunk at the Blue Norther

saloon and turned a poker card or two. Such was his entertainment.

As Ben paused near the bottomlands to water the roan, he glanced at the declining sun. Maybe it would be better to rest a night before pushing on. A jack-rabbit was the decider. He picked it off with a single shot, then off-saddled and skinned it with his Bowie to supplement his supper. When he rolled into his blankets staring at the stars the face of Colly Wells eluded him.

Mid-morning next day, he spotted Rocking Y punchers. Closer by, two riders emerged from the line shack. Using his glass he identified Jensen and the foreman, Dan Fallows. He coddled the roan forward.

'Mr Jensen. Dan.' He rested a hand casually on the saddle horn. 'How's the branding coming along?'

Fallows delivered a curt nod. 'When I got back from Bleak after looking for hands, I found you missing.'

Jensen was scowling. 'I know I said you'd be welcome back, Ben, but why this soon? You look like you've been roughed up.'

Ben tipped back his hat. 'Coupla things happened. First, I ran into some jaspers burning our calves with a Cut Circle iron.' As he explained, Jensen grew more attentive.

'Cut Circle? But Milt Lucas's spread has good repute.'

'Doubt if these were Lucas's men. And they'd had problems. A shot hoss; a shot man.' Ben added details, mentioning names.

Fallows wiped his face on his bandana. 'I've heard of McCabe. But as a gunman; not a cattleworker.'

'Most of 'em seemed green with cattle.'

Jensen frowned and looked at Fallows. 'Would you expect Lucas to deal with buzzards like these?'

'No, but his ramrod might. Rawlings could have struck some deal to take ready-branded stock. When Lucas comes to sell, Rawlings profits by some side-arrangement.'

The ranch boss sighed with irritation. 'So what next?'

'Oughtn't we to notify the marshal?' Fallows ventured.

Jensen snorted. 'The days Charlie Priest would take a posse after rustlers are gone. Priest by name, priest by nature.' He swung his glare on to Ben. 'I take it you ain't found your brother yet? Thought not. So what's the second thing that's happened?'

Ben gave a modest grin. 'I chanced to meet a young woman yon side of Buffalo Skulls. By some fluke she's seeking Frank as well. I wanted to check if he'd been here.'

Jensen glanced the query at Fallows who shook his head.

'Why here?' the rancher asked. 'Is he looking for you?'

'Doubt it. But this woman thinks he was making for Bleak. He's in trouble.' Ben explained what he knew. 'She don't know yet that we're brothers. I'd like to find him before she does.'

'The Rocking Y ain't a hideout for wanted men,' Jensen rasped with a grimace. 'Where've you left this woman?'

'She rode on to Bleak to check with the marshal.'

The rancher's lip gave a cynical twitch. 'We're gonna have Charlie Priest thinking his big day's arrived.'

Fallows was grinning. 'If she don't know you're brothers, that could take some living down if you see her again. Pretty, is she? You got an eye for her?'

'Maybe.' Ben stiffened his legs into the stirrups. 'Maybe I ain't saying.'

Jensen made a dismissive flourish. 'Ben, this brother's your own affair. Meantime – are you rejoining us?'

Ben shifted uncomfortably. 'I'd still like to find Frank first. Maybe I'll take a look into Bleak myself.'

'Stay here a night first. Ming Lee can roust you some cutlets.'

'Thanks, Mr Jensen.' Ben took stock of himself. 'I wouldn't mind resting my hoss till morning.'

'Yeah, you're fond of that roan.' Jensen raised a hand. 'Then here's my suggestion. Tomorrow make your enquiries. Also tell Priest about the rustlers. Tell him I'll be in the day after, branding permitting. We need action. Him and his stiff muscles ... Time he turned in his badge.' Jensen paused. 'Will you be putting up in Bleak tomorrow night?'

'Could be.' Ben glanced down at his scorched sleeve. 'Might buy myself a new coat and shirt.'

Fallows glanced slyly at Jensen. 'Sounds like this woman has impressed him if he's throwing those rags off his back.'

'A work shirt,' Ben qualified. With a righteous grimace, he turned the roan for the Rocking Y cookhouse.

When Clipper awoke it took him a while to get his bearings. Beyond a grimy window, dawn light was creeping through clouds as ragged as a sheep's fleece. Then he remembered.

He was in the Bleak rooming house. Doc Mason had bandaged his head but before riding off with Lou and Pierre had ordered Clipper to stay on here. This had been his second night.

Clipper eased back the blankets. He was alone. This was surely his chance to break free. His hoss should be in the livery. He could recall the doc telling Lou to leave it there.

He dragged his pants up over his long johns,

cinched them with his rawhide belt, and fumbled for his boots. He wedged his coonskin hat carefully over the bandage. Gathering his poncho, he sneaked into the chilly passage. He didn't know who he owed for meals, and didn't care. All he'd paid for was a new bandana. The dealer had brought it over yesterday.

Amid a smell of stale leftovers he entered the kitchen. He was gonna be hungry soon. He lifted two quarters of pie from a dish and wrapped them into his bandana. He could do with some coffee and he had no revolver, but he daren't waste time.

The street was deserted. The drowsy livery hostler asked no questions. Clipper raked up a ten-spot to pay for horse-feed. Mounting up was a struggle, but he made it. He set the horse walking along behind the buildings.

Which way? Any way free of McCabe. The crisp air made him yearn for his sheep-herding days back in Wyoming.

A mile west down the Sparville road he saw two riders coming up at a leisurely trot. Clipper screwed up his eyes to focus on them. A checkered Nebraskan coat; a gingery thatch ... In his vacant stomach a knot of dismay began to tighten and twist. He reined in and waited.

Lou was in front, but Pierre spoke first.

'Clipper, where the hell d'you think you're going?'

Clipper's jaw sagged, but words refused to form. A drool of spittle travelled down his whiskery chin.

'McCabe wants you,' Lou said. 'To look after Renny.'

Renny ... Clipper's well-being crumbled. How in hell's name could he have forgotten about Renny?

As they turned their mounts Clipper meekly fell in between them. His head was spinning and starting to hurt again.

# FOUR

Ben left the Rocking Y around noon and took close on three hours to reach Bleak Springs. He cantered the roan along the main street, picking through wagon tracks in the claggy mud.

There were few folk about. Two men sitting on a bench. An old timer in a rocker puffing at a corncob. Even in raw Montana there were those who upheld a siesta tradition.

The Blue Norther saloon sounded quiet. Ben passed the rooming house, assorted derelicts, traders and empty lots. He reached the livery stable at the end where he put up the roan.

'I'll be here till tomorrow,' he told Jimmy the hostler, and asked him to sort out a bag of best oats. As he slid the Springfield from its scabbard he noticed a black mare in one of the stalls. 'That one been here long?'

'Coupla days. Young woman asked to rest it.'

'She's in Bleak?'

'She hired another hoss to ride to her homestead. She'll be back maybe tomorrow.'

Ben walked back to the pineboard-fronted rooming house. He took a spare, left his belongings, and crossed to the store to pick up a few essentials including a supply of Bull Durham. He went along to the clothier's. Davison, the bluff tradesman with a droopy moustache, was pushing stubby logs into a pot-bellied stove in the centre of the floor space. Ben gave him a nod.

'Howdy. Can you sell me a vest and shirt? Maybe a coat?'

'Sure.' Davison rubbed his hands on his apron and retreated behind his counter. He pulled a stack of garments forward. 'Take a look. Find something you like.'

Ben floundered through them till he felt he was checking a deck for marked pasteboards. He made his selection.

'That's what I like,' the storeman approved. 'A man who don't dicker. These ranchers' wives spend hours choosin' a ribbon.' He glanced Ben over. 'You been in a range fire?'

'Branding fire. I got dragged into an argument.'

'Some argument.' Davison glanced at the shelves. 'You ain't interested in hats or bandanas? I sold a bandana yesterday to a beat-up old drifter, but the hats don't move. Tried one on him to replace his grubby coonskin, but he had a bandaged head and said it mightn't fit.'

'Coonskin and bandage?' Ben came alert. 'What was he like?'

'Fat, whiskery and unwashed. He sent over from the rooming house. Doc Mason had told him to rest. His talk was mighty garbled.'

'Is he still in Bleak?'

'I heard he slipped out early. He told me he wanted to break from a bunch of riders who'd hauled some hombre through a fire. Hey – did I say something funny?'

'Damn right. I'm the hombre they hauled.'

'Well, I'll be danged.' The storeman chewed on this for a moment. 'If it was me, I'd be making 'em pay for the shirt.'

'Thanks for the sympathy,' Ben said sourly. 'I'm hoping they'll pay for more than just a shirt.'

'Yeah? Watch you don't walk into trouble. You

want these items wrapping?'

'No. I'll be changing into 'em shortly.'

Ben peeled off some bills. He hoped his bed for the night was not the one Clipper had slept in.

Resting in his room, Ben began to think of his brother. Was it sense to assume Frank would shrug off trouble and return to ranch work? The sooner he could locate him, the better.

Ben swung off the bed and began to freshen up at the washstand. He shaved cautiously, scraping round his abrasions. Not a task he would have trusted to a barber even if Bleak Springs had one. Maybe he should get himself checked by Doc Mason. This rate, he was gonna take longer to heal than a brand on a steer. And perhaps he could ask the doc about Clipper.

With his new shirt donned he descended to seek a meal. The food in the eats house was prepared by a plump Chinese who rolled out pie dough with a bourbon bottle. But it was palatable. When Ben wiped off his mouth he felt ready to face the world.

He strolled out, the boardwalk resounding under his boot heels. He leant on a post while he built himself a smoke, struck a lucifer on the hitch rail and lit up. There was a nip in the air and the sun, cupped by the hills, threw long building shadows towards him. A buggy rumbled past. Across the street an old-timer was carrying a bucket of chicken feed. A dog wandered around, sniffing. Bleak Springs in the tail of afternoon.

A short way down, Charlie Priest stepped from his office and began to paste up a handbill outside his door. Ben glimpsed the word '*WANTED*' but was too far away to discern details. Priest dumped his pastepot back inside then came sauntering along, inhaling the air as though he owned it. Ben stopped him.

'Got a minute, marshal?'

Priest paused. From under a bruised brown hat he turned a weathered face at Ben. Shaggy brows canopied his steely eyes. His bushing moustache was tobacco-stained and his badge looked like it had been dropped in the mud and never recleaned.

'Always got a minute,' Priest said amicably. He tucked a thumb into his vest pocket. 'You're Rocking Y, ain't you?'

'Was. Ben Galliard – I rode out a few days ago.'

'Galliard? A young woman rode in coupla days back looking for a Galliard. She came to ask me about it.'

'Colly Wells, yeah. She's seeking my brother, Frank.'

'In trouble, ain't he? Busted jail at Sparville, she said.'

'He went there to try his luck. I'm seeking him myself.'

'Well, he ain't been here.'

'No? ... Then I got a message from Mr Jensen. He's aimin' to ride in tomorrow to discuss the rustling.'

'Uh-huh.' The marshal nodded, contemplating. 'That all?'

'All?' Ben removed the cigarette from his lips. 'It ain't that casual. Some stockraisers are getting riled. And I already met some of these thieves at close quarters.'

'You have?' Priest motioned towards a wall bench. They seated themselves in the waning sunlight. 'Any idea who?'

'Some. The leader's called McCabe. Rides a claybank.' Ben threw in more names. 'They were branding Rocking Y stock with a Cut Circle iron. Clipper was in Bleak last night, consulting Doc Mason –'

'Say, hold on. You gotta provide more than a string of names.' Priest turned his head to stare at Ben. 'I ain't heard none of those linked with Cut Circle. McCabe rings a bell, but I thought he was more of a sour-minded go-getter —'

'It don't alter what I saw. I was lucky to pull clear of the shootout.'

'Shootout? How many of these villains have you killed?'

'Ain't sure I killed any. Though the one called Renny was wiltin' fast. There were nine of 'em.'

Priest puffed through his moustache. 'But where'm I supposed to look for 'em?' He sounded drained of enthusiasm.

Ben suppressed a prickle of irritation. 'Hell, marshal, what more d'you want? McCabe was running the stock to Cut Circle. He was due to meet others at Blackfoot Bluff.'

'That ain't conclusive.'

'You mean you'd rather just poke around Bleak?'

Priest studied Ben's features through slit eyelids. 'You look like you need patching up. What you been treating that face with — prickly pear?'

Ben ignored the taunt. He stifled his pique. He knew when his efforts were being wasted.

'Anything else?' Priest had frosted over as though the topic of rustling was now dismissed.

'Nope. If you ain't seen my brother ...'

'How big a trouble's he in? That woman said something 'bout her grandfather being shot.'

'I only know her version. Frank was jailed for killing her Grandpa with a scattergun. But that ain't Frank's style.'

'Men change.' The marshal looked at him hard. 'If your brother does turn up here I might have to arrest him.'

Ben smirked in silence, then said: 'So that's about as useful as you'll get?' He flicked his home-rolled out into the mud. 'How long since you did arrest anyone, marshal?'

Priest blustered. 'Now don't start that sort of talk with me. You know I can only play the hands I'm dealt.'

'Holding your lawbadge tight into your chest?'

'Look, son ...' Relenting, Priest spread his arms. 'Sparville's out of my area. Let Sheriff Quayle deal with it.'

'And if Sparville sends a dodger saying Frank Galliard's a wanted man – what then?'

The marshal hedged. 'Then I'm holding a different hand.'

Rooftop shadows were beginning to touch them. Ben pulled himself up from the bench. 'Time I consulted Doc Mason.'

The doc's place was a south-facing plain-front with a pineboard shingle: '*Dr L. MASON – SURGERY.*' Ben walked in and sat down while Doc finished washing his hands.

'Could you check this over?' Ben touched his scorched and abraded cheek. 'I clashed with some rustlers.'

Mason turned up his two lamps. He was a stern-looking gent in a floral waistcoat, with dark pouches below his eyes. 'It don't look too serious,' he said, inspecting. He applied some salve. After examining Ben's other grazes, he pronounced him fit.

'I believe you treated one of the men I tangled with,' Ben said. 'Name of Clipper. He'd clouted his head.'

'Clipper? He rode in three nights ago with two other men – called Lou and Pierre. Late – I'd just locked up. I put a dressing on him. He left the rooming house this morning.'

'I ain't that concerned for his health. Just

wondering where these jaspers might be. Another of 'em – Renny – could be holed up some place with a nasty wound.'

Mason stroked his chin. 'I'll tell you this much. Clipper's two companions weren't keen on him staying in Bleak. And they were here to take me to Blackfoot Bluff. Renny was bedded in a wagon there nursing a bullet, too weak to move.'

'They persuaded you to ride out?'

Mason released a chilly smile. 'They were persuasive men. As was their boss-man, McCabe. Digging .45 lead and splintered rib out of Renny's chest under firebrand lighting weren't ideal surgery. But I seldom ask questions.'

Ben did not think Lou and Pierre had been among the original party. Maybe McCabe had met up with extras.

'Did you see any cattle about at Blackfoot?'

'No. They didn't admit to any.'

'They probably shifted the few they'd taken. But Charlie Priest won't do much. His range-riding days are over.'

The doc sighed. 'Don't be too hard on Charlie. Confidentially, it ain't just his leg. He once had a slight stroke.'

'I thought he took a tumble from a hoss.'

'That was earlier. But he still wouldn't chuck in his badge.' Mason began to sort through his stack of ointments.

'Renny seems to be getting special attention,' Ben said, buttoning up his shirt. 'What state did you leave him in?'

Mason considered. 'Touch and go. I advised McCabe to get him under a roof, but he seemed more interested in having him fit enough to talk. Maybe you can explain that?'

'Nope. It's kinda mystifying.'

Ben felt for his billfold to pay the fee. Picking up

his hat he left the doctor to his brooding.

Clipper huddled by the campfire, warming his fingers on the mug of coffee that someone had grudgingly provided. He was still bone-weary after riding back from Bleak Springs.

It had taken him ages to remember those mangled pie quarters wrapped in his bandana. The coffee was helping to swill them down.

McCabe came striding across, the tip of his cheroot brightening as he drew on it. He loomed gaunt over Clipper.

'So who else might you have spoken to?' he asked.

Clipper fingered his bandaged brow. 'The sawbones. He gave me this dressing –'

'Never mind the sawbones.' McCabe quelled an exasperated sigh. 'Did you tell anyone about Renny and the work he once did in Sparville? ... God in hell, you remember Renny?'

Clipper stared vacantly. McCabe swung away in disgust and began talking to Chub who was checking a rope for frays.

'I wouldn't fret,' Chub muttered. 'Clipper ain't a threat.'

'Then why d'you think I wanted him brought back? Not just to look after Renny. I didn't want rumour spread around Bleak by some half-wit sheep-shearer.'

Clipper felt churned in the guts to hear them discussing him this way.

Chub grunted: 'It would've bin a helluva lot simpler if Lou had dropped Clipper off his hoss before he ever got to Bleak. What was wrong with keeping that doc here anyway?'

'To care for Renny? I was glad to see the back of him – suspicious bastard. Clipper's the most valuable in getting Renny to talk, assuming he comes round.'

Chub looked dubious. He set the coiled rope aside. 'You don't reckon Renny might have told Clipper already –?'

'I want to hear it from Renny.' McCabe fed Chub an icy stare. 'I don't want garble from a sheepherder. Besides, if Slim Cricklewood hears it from Renny's own mouth, it could convince him about the new plan. He should be here by tomorrow.'

The discussion droned on. Clipper dimly wondered if he should drag himself up on to the wagon, check how comfortable Renny was lying on his tarp among those explosives.

He must show willing, to stay alive himself.

# FIVE

As Ben crossed from Doc Mason's towards Priest's office he glanced over the Blue Norther batwings. The custom within looked thin even for Bleak.

A lamp hung outside the marshal's door. Ben paused to read the handbill on the panel. Five thousand dollars reward for Henry 'Slim' Cricklewood, wanted for robbery and murder. A failed bank raider, Cricklewood had taken to robbing stages, some as far afield as Yellowstone country. Skilled with a gun, despite an eye-cast. Ben studied the facial sketch. Aquiline nose under a flat-brimmed hat; tight slitted eyes revealing the cast. Ben tapped on the door and walked in.

Priest glanced up from trimming a lamp. He eyed Ben's ointmented cheek. 'You've spoken to Doc Mason?'

'Yeah. Did you know two men took him to McCabe's camp to dig the slug out of Renny?' Ben leant beside the gunrack. 'Right now though I'm concerned for Frank. Musta missed him some place.'

Priest sat down in his rail-backed chair, opened his desk drawer and propped a foot on it. 'He could have ridden straight through. Or maybe he's run into that Wells woman by now. She could make trouble for your brother. I'm speaking as an experienced lawman.'

'Yeah? I ain't exactly ignorant of the law myself.

Used to be an interest of mine. Still is.'

'Bunkhouse lawyer, eh?' Tilting back, the marshal regarded Ben from under his battered hat brim. 'Then what d'you make of this lot?' He gestured towards a stack of handbills on the desk.

'Slim Cricklewood, failed bank raider? I been lookin' at the one you pasted up. An arch-enemy of yours?'

'Hell, no. I only ever saw him once, when he hot-hoofed from a stage job near Livingston. Taking a stage is easier than tackling a town bank. Banks are too sturdy, unless you can bribe someone to leave the strongroom ajar. And if that can happen' – Priest gave a snorting laugh – 'it ain't a place I'd put my money.'

Ben tapped the dodgers. 'They've sent a hell of a wad.'

'I'll spread 'em around in good time. Stage only dropped 'em off this morning. I ain't met a situation yet in Bleak that demanded fast action.'

Priest's eyes had glazed over. He remained with his leg propped on the drawer, showing no inclination to stir.

'You still ain't said what happens if Frank turns up.'

'No, 'cause I've had no notification.'

'No chance of you contacting Sparville about it?'

'Three days ridin'? What d'ya take me for?' The marshal placed his hat down; the lamp threw silvery streaks into his hair. 'Tarnation, the way you pester I'm beginning to think you want your brother in the hoosegow.'

'Forget it then, marshal.' Ben released a grin. 'I wouldn't presume to know your job.'

Priest began to ply his hat brim into a better shape. 'No hard feelings, son. So what's your next move?'

'Time I tried the whisky in the Blue Norther.'

Horses were hitched outside the saloon. The air was keener as Ben strode down the gloomy boardwalk and pushed through the batwings. Billy, the balding barkeep, stood polishing a glass. Sconce-lamps penetrated the cigarette haze to illuminate the wall portraits of theatrical ladies.

Three men in flat-crowned hats and sombre garb lounged at the bar sharing a bottle. From the ironwork in their gunbelts they looked to be more than the average saddletramp. The large mirror behind the bar reflected the scene.

Ben advanced leisurely and nodded to Billy. 'Bourbon,' he said. He glanced casually at the trio then savoured his drink, wondering if Billy knew anything of his brother. Hearing a cackle, he noticed the tall aquiline man in the middle of the threesome staring at the top of the mirror.

'Wa-all now, Timbo – don't some folk ask for trouble?' The man nudged the stubbly companion on his right.

Without looking, Ben knew what he meant. Some lettering under the ornate frame said: *WHEN THROWING TABLES – BUST THE BOTTLES, NOT THE MIRROR.* Everyone around knew of this motto; so these three had to be strangers.

As Billy disappeared down his cellar to fetch a crate, Ben watched them leering in amusement. The sharp-featured one was mean-lipped with untidy sideburns. He was packing a brace of pearl-handled Colts. Timbo was stockier, with a hardtack face. The third was younger, fair crinkly hair pushing his hat off.

Timbo grinned impudently. 'Sounds like it's an invitation.'

Ben felt obliged to speak. 'They say that notice went up five years back. The mirror's still in one piece.'

The trio glowered at Ben. The thin one spoke: 'That won't last for ever.' As Ben crossed gazes with the man's reflection, one eye seemed to look over his shoulder.

Ben adjusted weight, leaning on the bar. 'Story goes the previous mirror got shattered in a fight. When the owner bought a replacement, the notice appeared. Billy'll tell you.'

'Tell 'em what?' Billy emerged to dump a full crate down. Guessing the topic, he warmed to the tale. 'Yeah, his humour paid off. That mirror's had a charmed life.'

The trio listened in surly silence. Ben continued to assess the thin man through half-closed eyelids, comparing the aquiline features with those he'd seen on Charlie Priest's handbills.

In a long slow swallow Ben drained his glass and set it down. 'You fellers just passin' through?' he asked.

Timbo turned to look Ben over. 'Why? What's it to you?'

Ben shrugged. 'Nothing. Thought I saw you ride in from the east; wondered if you were heading for the mines.'

'Do we look like miners?' the thin one grated. 'Hey, bar-dog. How far we gotta ride to reach Blackfoot Bluff?'

Billy paused in his bar-wiping. 'Four hours, I guess.'

'It's got to be where I said,' the crinkly youth told the thin man. 'McCabe should have picked an easier spot.'

'Dry up, Curly. We're stuck with meeting him as agreed.'

As the trio lapsed into muted conversation, Ben chipped in lazily: 'You should reach Blackfoot in just over three.'

Timbo stared him in the face. 'Who asked you to

listen in?'

'I never listen in.' Ben pushed his glass aside. 'I just got good hearing.'

'Slim, I told you,' Curly said, sulking, 'we should be talking in a private room.'

'Curly, hush your mouth,' the lean one snarled. To Ben, he said: 'What do you know about Blackfoot Bluff?'

'I've driven cattle that way. That's about all.'

The man stared for several seconds as Ben eased from the bar. Sauntering out, Ben glanced idly up at the room doors along the landing. One had just opened, revealing a tall man about to descend the stairs. Something familiar registered; but Ben was already thrusting through the batwings.

Right then his concern was to find Charlie Priest.

The marshal was just emerging from his office with a fistful of Cricklewood handbills. Ben pushed him back inside.

'Hey, what in tarnation – ?' Priest blustered.

'You ain't dishing those out now? Slap one on Billy's bar and you could be in trouble. Cricklewood's in the saloon.'

Priest braked as though winded. 'Cricklewood? Here?'

'Beyond doubt. Him and two other gunnies, Curly and Timbo. Riding in from the west they wouldn't pass that dodger you stuck up outside.'

Priest wallowed in disbelief. 'You sure?'

'Three whiskey drinkers. First time in the Norther.'

'How in hell d'you know that?'

'Got to be. They'd never seen the notice before about bustin' Billy's mirror.' At the marshal's dazed look, Ben added: 'They were talking of meeting up with McCabe.'

Priest leant on the chair back where his gunbelt

was looped. 'I already dropped the first of these flyers in on Billy an hour back. He laid it on the shelf under the bar.'

His fingers touched the gunbelt. Spurred into decision, he began to strap it on. Ben felt a prod of anxiety.

'What you planning to do?' he asked, watching.

'Arrest Cricklewood. Ain't that why you came back?'

'I came to warn you.' Ben clutched at his arm. 'If you go waving a dodger under Billy's nose with Cricklewood standing there supping bourbon you could be biting the floorboards.'

'Dammit, I'm a lawman.' Priest shook himself free as some of his old fire blazed. 'No Slim Cricklewood's gonna ride over my town.' Florid with rancour he fumbled to fasten the buckle.

Ben waited, wishing for some easy way out. 'There's four guns among 'em. Cricklewood's strapping a brace of pearl-handleds.'

Checking his hammer mechanism with stiff fingers, Priest paused and glared. 'What are you trying to tell me?'

'Durn it, I'm telling you to stay alive. You need help.'

The marshal hesitated, shoulders sagging. 'You offering?'

'I don't see anyone else coming forward. But wouldn't it be safer to wait until he leaves the saloon?'

'We ain't got time to wait.' Priest raked a hand into a drawer and came out clutching a glint of metal. 'Put that on.'

'Deputy star? You swearing me in?'

'There ain't time for formalities,' barked Priest.

Seconds later Ben had the badge pinned home.

'That Colt of yours loaded?' The marshal yanked the door open. 'We'll play this hand the way it's dealt.'

They trod along the walk until they could see into the saloon. Ben kept close by the marshal's side.

Cricklewood and his two gunnies had taken a table near the centre of the floor. A fourth man had joined them, seated with his back to the entrance. They were engrossed at cards.

Cricklewood was on the left. Ben took in the aquiline profile. Curly sat facing the batwings. Timbo occupied a chair opposite Cricklewood. All four players remained unsuspecting.

'The poker game,' Ben muttered to Priest. 'Are you sure you wouldn't rather let 'em all come out first?'

'And how long's that gonna take? Besides ...'

As Priest gave a nudge, Ben followed his glance. Along the bar Doc Mason was purchasing a bottle. Billy had unfolded a handbill to stick up by his mirror. As he broke off to serve a cowpoke rattling an empty glass, Mason reached to study the dodger and went suddenly tense.

'The Doc's spotted them.' Priest moved to go in.

'Wait,' Ben hissed; he caught the marshal's sleeve. 'That player with his back to us ...' It was the man he had glimpsed on the landing; a face he should have known. Now the man's head turned slightly, allowing Ben a glimpse of a small scar by the left sideburn. 'It's my brother, Frank.'

Charlie Priest stood rooted to the boardwalk.

'Your brother? The one who's wanted in Sparville?'

'He's only playing cards. Let me speak with him first.'

Priest champed at a stray whisker of moustache, considering the issues: the arresting of Cricklewood, and possibly the taking of Frank Galliard.

Ben thought he detected a flicker of unfulfilled ambition crossing the marshal's face.

Priest said, 'What you aiming to do, talk him clear of that poker table?'

'I just want him to know I'm here.'

The marshal relented. 'Speak to him then. But leave Cricklewood to me. I'll be right behind you.'

As Ben thrust at the batwings he felt a stark doubt. Could he be sure Frank was not in cahoots with these men?

There were outward changes – black hat, hand-stitched boots, tartaned vest; all had hindered recognition. But had the man changed? At least he did not seem to be packing a gun.

Ben halted a yard behind the chair. 'Frank,' he said.

The familiar face turned in a quick glance. 'Holy heifers! Where you rode in from?' Frank began to stand, but remembering his poker etiquette he froze on the seat, glancing an apology at the others. 'It's the kid brother,' he grinned.

'Don't let me interrupt,' Ben said, aware of the pique on Cricklewood's face, 'but when you can break from the game –'

'You'd like to talk? Yeah, sure.'

Behind Priest the batwings flapped shut. Cricklewood was already appraising the marshal. His attention flitted to Mason who was joshing the handbill with Billy. The barkeep stared, mouth parted in disbelief.

'If you're still playing,' Cricklewood gritted at Frank, 'tell your kid brother to wait his turn.'

He had clearly missed nothing. His free hand tensed, fingernails scraping at the tabletop. Priest forced himself past Ben to confront the gunman.

'Henry Slim Cricklewood,' he intoned. 'There's a call out for your arrest. As marshal of this town, I'm taking you in.' He rested a hand by his Colt. 'You gonna come peaceably?'

Cricklewood broke into a tight-lipped drawl. 'Marshal, I'm all set to call a man's bluff.' He glanced at Ben, his cast-eyed stare coasting to the deputy's badge. 'Been using the tin-snips, kid? You weren't wearing that star before. Ain't you gonna let us finish this hand, marshal?'

Priest gave a firm shake of his head. Ben edged a step nearer. 'The marshal wants you along. Pronto.'

The others had barely stirred. Frank was immobile. Curly seemed to be waiting for Timbo to move. Timbo sat touching cards to his chin, one hand resting near his rolled-up gunbelt.

'You shiftin' or ain't you?' Priest's fingers cupped the butt of his .45. 'Or do we do this at gunpoint?'

'Never decline an invitation.' Cricklewood began to slide his chair back. 'Hand ain't worth a wooden nickel anyway.'

He was still holding the fan of pasteboards. Then – no longer. Before the cards hit the floor he flashed into movement. Flame and lead blasted into Charlie's Priest's chest.

The marshal had just cleared leather. He staggered back against the batwings and crashed out into the mud-sodden roadway – leaving Ben fighting for life.

As Cricklewood's second gun appeared, Ben fired. Cricklewood twisted, dropping a Colt, to sprawl against the bar-rail. Ben wrenched round at Timbo who was hefting his iron.

'Don't try it!' As Timbo ignored him, Ben ripped a slug through the gunnie's rib-cage. Timbo fell, shedding his weapon. As Curly jerked up a squat Peacemaker, Frank rammed the table into the youngster's groin, jolting his aim. Cards and whiskey glasses scattered. Frank rolled aside into a huddle.

The guns of Ben and Curly roared together. Ben heard singing lead. Curly yelped; his Peacemaker span free. Tripping, he hit the cuspidor. Ben lunged back, straddle-legged, commanding the saloon. He glimpsed Timbo kneeling, dripping blood, groping for Cricklewood's Colt. Ben waited. Timbo's eyes rolled upwards. He toppled. The unfired gun thudded to the floor.

A scuffling jerked Ben round. Curly was up, stumbling out through the batwings. Ben heard him galloping away.

A Boot Hill silence cocooned the Blue Norther. Gunsmoke stank of death. Ben shuddered. He holstered his Colt and wiped the sweat from his jaw, allowing his focus to broaden.

Customers were unfurling from cover. Frank was dusting off floorboard grit. Doc Mason poked his head out from the rear arch. Ignoring the two sprawled gunmen, he tramped outside. He was back in moments, looking grim. 'The marshal's dead.'

'Hell.' Ben felt choked wordless. He turned aside, fingers flexing, while Mason checked the gunnies. 'Two more dead'uns here.' Ben stood watching, nauseated by his handiwork.

Billy came through the barflap. 'Billy, you'd better contact Mr Cousins,' Mason said. 'And somebody ask Pinebox Keel to bring a coffin board for the marshal.'

# SIX

Cousins the saloon proprietor was a large man in an ornate jacket styled like a riverboat gambler's. On arrival he began to serve up advice on where to put the dead gunhawks.

'The outhouse, Billy? Nothing in there to spoil.'

'Suits me,' Billy agreed.

Mason came back in from the street where a group was gathering to help with the marshal. 'Anybody else hit?' Satisfied, he turned to watch the volunteers carrying the gunmen's bodies out.

Cousins attempted a joke: 'Now you know what's meant by hefting a dead weight.' This eased the tension, but Ben would have given a gold seam for none of this to have happened.

He joined his brother who was languishing on the bar. 'Frank, you sure as hell took your time diving for cover.'

'I'll tell you something, kiddo.' Frank pointed a finger at him. 'A moving target draws the gunfire.'

'What you doing here anyway, gambling with that mob?'

'They'd only just dealt me in.' Frank stuck a thumb in the top of his pants. 'I rode in from Sparville thinking maybe I'd work on one of the spreads.'

'You mean you ducked out of Sparville to escape trouble.' As Frank raised his eyebrows, Ben explained: 'I met a young woman called Colly

Wells. She told me about it.'

Frank merely shrugged. 'There weren't much future in Sparville. Old Uncle Denzil – he's dead of pneumonia.'

'Colly Wells mentioned that too. Where are you staying?'

Frank nodded up towards the landing. 'Right here.' He broke off as Mason straddled a chair to face him.

'I take it you weren't one of those gunmen?'

'He's my brother,' Ben said, rankling a little.

'That a fact?' Mason registered surprise. 'So was it Charlie Priest's idea to tackle Cricklewood? With your help?' He nodded at Ben's badge.

'Yeah.' Ben's hand strayed up to finger the star. He began to see problems arising. 'So what now?'

Mason glanced toward the batwings. 'That sounds like the coffin board arriving. So now we see that Charlie's handled with respect.' Turning his back on Frank, he led Ben outside.

With the aid of three stalwarts Pinebox Keel, undertaker, had just lifted the body on to the board. Ben gazed upon the lifeless face while Mason gingerly checked the pockets.

'Smoking tackle. No keys. He didn't lock his office?'

'No. He was too anxious to get down here.'

They covered the body with a blanket and laid the marshal's bruised hat upon his chest. When he had been carried away Mason looked at Ben. 'Does that badge mean you'll carry on helping?'

'Can do.' Any other answer would have been unacceptable.

'Come back inside then.' Mason led Ben through to the outhouse where the dead gunmen lay. After scanning their wounds, he said: 'Charlie would have checked the pockets and locked their possessions up in his office.'

'You asking me to do it?'

'You're wearing the badge. Here, I'll help. Go ask Billy for a couple of cartons for their bits and pieces.'

Presently the meagre belongings lay in two cardboard boxes marked 'Cricklewood' and 'Timbo.' There was little of importance. Ben studied two scraps of paper from Cricklewood's pocket.

'This one's a note abut meeting McCabe, the rustler boss. The other looks like stage schedules from Sparville.'

'Maybe that was Cricklewood's intention. Robbing a stage.'

Ben stroked his chin. 'I'm wondering about Curly, the one who rode out. He could be heading to join McCabe.'

'There ain't much we can do tonight. I reckon our town council ought to meet tomorrow. To discuss things.'

'Mr Jensen talked about riding in tomorrow.'

'Not before time.' Mason closed the outhouse door behind them. 'I'd better show you where Charlie kept his keys and such.'

'What about the stuff you raked from his pockets?'

'I'll take that in hand for now.' Re-entering the saloon, Mason paused. 'Now, somewhere I bought me a bottle ...' He scooped it up as Billy shoved it across the bar.

As they made for the batwings, Billy called after Ben: 'Thanks anyway, cowboy.'

Ben grimaced. 'Gunplay ain't my favourite pastime.'

'I mean thanks for shooting straight.' Billy jerked a thumb over his shoulder. 'I still got me a one-piece mirror.'

Inside Priest's office Mason sat down, shook his head and sighed. 'Charlie must sure have been in some hurry. Did he swear you in?'

'He kinda rushed me.' Ben sat on a corner of the desk and rooted out his makings. 'When I offered to help, he stuck this star on me.' He began to roll a smoke, wondering how he was to face the shattered community of Bleak Springs.

'What an all-fired mess.' Mason reached under the lamp glass to adjust the wick. 'We should have talked Charlie out of his badge long ago.'

As Ben snapped his thumbnail on a match to light up, Mason rummaged into a drawer and produced two spectacle cases. 'Coupla pairs of glasses. He never wore the damned things. With his eyes I wouldn't have fancied my chances in a gunfight.'

Ben blew smoke, watching it curl around the lamp. 'You saying I did wrong by Charlie, prodding him into a fight?'

'Did you prod him?'

'A little. It was a marshal's responsibility.'

'Yeah, well ... It's done now.'

Ben dropped the Cricklewood handbills into the trash can. 'You don't recall Clipper saying anything more? Or Renny? Or anyone else at McCabe's camp?'

'You mean, concerning Cricklewood and McCabe? ... Not a lot. You know Clipper was a sheepman? As for Renny — I couldn't help feeling he had more of a townsman's background.'

'I suppose that's better than stinking of sheep.'

'Or cattlemen stinking of beeves.' Mason threw Ben a critical look. 'I never did figger why you waddies regard sheepmen as the scum of the earth.'

Ben shifted his feet, retracting. 'They've always gotten in cattlemen's way. A lesser breed. Unpopular.'

'Yeah? Well, all this friction saddens me.'

As Mason began to flick through Priest's notebook Ben stayed silent, feeling that he had been ticked off.

'Another thing,' Mason went on. 'If McCabe's men were genuine cow-reared, they'd be less likely to put up with Clipper. So don't that suggest some deeper bond? Maybe a big job in waiting. If you weren't so set against sheepmen, you might have realised this.'

Ben drew on his hand-rolled, pondering. 'I did kinda wonder. The rustling was a stop-gap.'

Mason slammed the drawer shut. 'Let's take a look round.'

They toured the empty cells, the living quarters, and back to the office. Mason found keys to a cupboard containing Colt and Remington handguns. Others fitted the cells and gunrack. Mason seemed satisfied.

'Where are you staying tonight?' he asked.

'The rooming house. Frank's booked in at the saloon.'

Mason thought for a moment. 'Then tonight we'll share things. I'll take charge of Charlie's keys. If I need a deputy, I'll come looking. Tomorrow, we'll decide what's to be done.'

As they went out Mason locked the door.

Ben entered the saloon across the freshy swabbed floor.

'That brother of mine around?'

Before Billy could answer, Frank emerged from the rear.

'Come on up, Ben. We can talk in private.'

Inside his room, Frank heeled the door shut and sat on the creaky bed. Ben took a chair by the washstand.

'So?' Frank surveyed Ben, their first relaxed chance to look at each other. 'What led you to Bleak

Springs?'

'Looking for you. You knew about Pa dying? Ma's wanting you back. He left a deskful of paperwork.'

Frank emitted a surly grunt. 'Ben, you know I ain't no pen-pusher. Can't someone else deal with it?'

'The others are ridin' and ropin'. I been tailing you over a year. Even spent a season on the Rocking Y.'

'You ain't exactly been rushin'.'

Ben shrugged. He studied his brother – a big-boned, rough-skinned man. Lazy, but one to be relied on in an emergency.

'About the Wells girl,' Ben said. 'She's been enquiring for you in Bleak.'

Frank looked concerned. 'I thought I'd shaken her off. I didn't expect her to be so persistent.'

'Right now she's visiting her folks. But you got one advantage. She don't know yet that we're brothers.'

Frank gave a curt laugh. 'She ain't gonna like it when she finds out. What's she told you? 'Cause it's her dead Grandpa, old Eli Dunn, that's back of all this.'

'She told me someone called Hayley saw you take a shotgun into his cabin; and the Sparville sheriff reckons you could have killed him, believing he'd stolen Uncle Denzil's gold.'

'They'd been pards, sure.' Frank sprawled back, hands clasped behind his head. 'But if Denzil had lost gold, it don't mean her Grandpa took it. Or that I went gunning for him, or stole any other gold that Eli had.'

'So what really happened, Frank? Did you kill her Grandpa?'

'My shotgun did, but I weren't there. Sheriff Quayle arrested me, but I picked his keybunch off him through the bars. Other than that, I'm pure and blameless.'

'But something must have happened. Ain't you any idea?'

Frank sighed. 'I left the shotgun in her Grandpa's cabin while I went to check his traps. When I got back he was dead. Buckshot wounds. Quayle jugged me on the strength of Hayley's say-so. The Wells woman chose to believe Quayle ... What the hell you doing wearing a law badge anyway?'

'Talked myself into it.'

'Then take the damned thing off.' Frank swung his feet to the floor. 'Anyway, you've no cause to worry. You're smarter now with a gun than when I taught you to shoot jack-rabbits. A right whelp you were then.' Frank gestured. 'Has someone been frying your face?'

'I ran into some rustlers led by a man called McCabe. Cricklewood had been due to meet him.'

'Sticking your neck out, ain't you? What if I'd been in cahoots with Cricklewood? Not just a fourth at poker.'

Ben fed his brother a critical look. 'Frank, I ain't misjudged you that much. As for the deputy badge – I'll be handing it in when the council meets in the morning.'

Clipper jolted awake and tightened his poncho against the cold. He peered at Renny who lay beside him, starlit and blanket-wrapped on the bed of the wagon. He was wondering what had roused him when above the snores of sleeping men he heard the hallooing of an approaching rider.

The lookout called: 'Who's riding in?'

'Curly Gleason.'

Clipper blinked across towards McCabe who was starting to peel from his bedroll. 'Let him forward,' McCabe ordered.

The rider dismounted. He looked young, dishevelled. His horse was flecked in sweat. McCabe crossed to greet him. Clipper could sense that something was wrong.

'Where are Cricklewood and Timbo?' McCabe demanded.

The agitated Curly shook his head. 'Snuffed out. Bleak Springs marshal tried to arrest Slim.'

'Jesus!' McCabe lapsed into cursing. 'How in hell —?'

Curly's broken explanation was lost on Clipper. The youth turned to the smouldering camp fire. 'Any hot drink in the pot?'

'Get him some coffee.'

McCabe began to pace. Disquiet spread as the other men roused to learn the news. Chub's voice muttered: 'Is this gonna throw us, McCabe? You said Slim'd be hard to replace.'

McCabe considered. 'It puts a new slant on things. I knew he'd take some persuading to change from stages, his proven targets. But if he's dead, he can't object.'

'So you'll be running this your way from now?'

McCabe nodded. 'This is what we've been nursing Renny for; him and those dynamite boxes. If anybody objects, say so now.'

The only response was a long silence.

Clipper lowered his head, listening for Renny's rasping breath. He straightened up, leaning dizzily on the boxes of explosive. Stooping like that set his brow thumping.

Yet Clipper derived a kind of stunted pride from knowing he was tending the key man. This somehow atoned for the way he was mistreated. Whatever the information was that McCabe wanted from Renny, it must be mighty crucial. But right now Renny was no more wordy than a stunned sheep.

McCabe turned to Lou and Pierre and as they rinsed their cups.

'How d'you two feel like riding on ahead to Sparville?'

'What – now?' Lou grumbled in dismay. 'What for?'

'A small task you can deal with.' McCabe went into details; they meant little to Clipper. As Lou and Pierre prepared to saddle up, McCabe's voice rose to address the others.

'Grab what sleep you can. We'll move out by sun-up.'

# SEVEN

The next morning Ben was out early. He found Davison flicking debris from his clothing store doorway with a broom.

'Do you know what time the council meets?'

'Soon, I guess. We meet in my store.' Davison leant on his broom. 'I hear you been dirtying that new shirt.'

'The shootout?' Ben nodded ruefully. He sauntered to the eating house to get his juices flowing with bacon and coffee. When he stepped back outside he saw Jensen and two other ranchers hitching their horses and talking to Doc Mason.

'I've been hearing what happened.' Jensen greeted him with concern. 'The council might want to talk to you later.'

As the council went into session Ben made for the saloon where Billy was swilling the boardwalk by his outer doors.

'If you're looking for your brother,' Billy said, 'he paid Mr Cousins what he owed then lit out early.'

Ben halted. 'The hell he has. Did he say where to?'

'Nope. Said he wanted to clear his lungs of gunsmoke.'

Ben clicked his tongue. He strode down to the livery to check with the hostler. A smell of fresh hay and manure drifted from the stalls.

'Jimmy, has my brother been in to collect his nag?'

'Big feller; small scar? He rode out some half hour back. That woman ain't been back for her mare either.' Jimmy noticed the deputy's badge. 'I hear we lost ourselves a marshal.'

'Yeah.' Ben nodded uninformatively and walked back up the warming street. Near the clothier's he saw Jensen beckoning.

'Can you come in, Ben? Council'd like a word.'

'Now? ... Durned brother of mine – I found him in Bleak last night and now he's vamoosed.'

Jensen seemed unconcerned. He led Ben into the clothier's.

Chairs had been arranged near the stove. Among those present, Ben noticed Cousins, Doc Mason and Sam Garner who managed the stage depot. Jensen pointed to a spare chair. Declining to sit, Ben propped his foot on it.

'Fact is, Ben,' said Jensen, 'we're in a quandary. We don't think the rustling's all that serious. Dan's visiting the Cut Circle to dicker with Lucas about our lost stock. But right now we're concerned about last night. I gather you put the law into practice in no uncertain way.'

Ben grunted with embarrassment. 'What's that supposed to mean? Charlie Priest's lying in a pine box.'

'Sad and unfortunate. But now we're seeking a replacement. And you seem to fit the requirements.'

'Me?' Ben slowly straightened up. 'Hey, hold your fire –'

'Ben, on my ranch you made a good tophand. But you ain't restricted to cow work. You kept a law book in the bunkhouse –'

'I never found time to read the damned thing. Look – why ain't you appointing a new marshal from the townsfolk?'

Mason cut in. 'It ain't that simple, Ben. We've

been racking our brains. We know you impressed Charlie.'

'Exaggeration. He hardly knew me.' But Ben could see all eyes upon him. He ran a finger around his bandana. 'Are you sure you know what you're letting yourselves in for?'

Cousins spoke, gruff and amiable. 'Ben, for me you've already proved your mettle. I'd be proud to have you marshal.'

'For what? Tramping the boardwalks like Charlie Priest?'

'Ben, I told you why he stuck to the town,' Mason implored. 'If it makes you happier we could still treat the appointment as temporary. But we want to know what Cricklewood and McCabe were hatching between 'em.'

'You're asking me to look into something McCabe ain't even done yet.'

'I know it's fanciful.' Mason nodded. 'By what I overheard at his camp, he could be making for Sparville.'

Ben began to roll a smoke. 'If I take on as marshal, it ain't 'cause of McCabe. It's 'cause I owe it to Charlie Priest.'

With a flicker of remorse, Cousins said: 'You don't owe Charlie any more than we do. You're simply the best choice.'

'And McCabe is the menace,' Jensen summed. 'That's why we want his plans in check.' He glanced at the others, inviting final questions.

Sam Garner asked: 'Where did you learn to shoot?'

'Texas mostly.' Ben scratched modestly at his cheek.

The council members seemed satisfied.

'Well, Ben?' Jensen glared. 'What do you say?'

Ben lit his smoke. He took his foot off the chair. If he followed McCabe towards Sparville he might also find a chance to learn more of the mess Frank was in.

'I guess I'll accept,' he said. 'For a while.'

As though to clinch agreement Jensen shook Ben's hand. Mason exchanged a marshal's badge for the deputy's on Ben's vest. 'You're wearing a dead man's star,' Jensen reminded him. Ben fingered it, conscious of its weight.

From the counter Mason tugged forward the cardboard box marked 'Cricklewood' and took out a tattered notebook.

'We found this in Cricklewood's saddlebag,' he said. 'It lists dates, places and sums of several thousand dollars. And those figures that you thought were stage schedules, we think they relate to gold deliveries from Sparville to places east.'

Garner said: 'There were no robberies on those dates, but the last of 'em ain't reached us yet. It's five days off.'

Ben stubbed his smoke. 'But wouldn't information on gold need to come from some reliable source in Sparville?'

Jensen planted a hand on the table. 'Ben, we think any threat to gold should be looked into. We reckon enquiries should be raised with the sheriff there, or the assay office.'

'And where's this gold robbery gonna take place?'

Mason flipped Cricklewood's notebook open. 'There's a mention of Sunstroke Rocks. That's near to Sparville. The same date's noted beside it, in five days; but with a question mark.'

Ben began to fan his face with his hat. 'So do we assume McCabe's taking over where Cricklewood left off?'

Mason tilted his head. 'Could be, 'specially if Curly joined him after hightailing out last night.'

He ruminated. 'In Charlie's office this morning I found an old flyer on McCabe. He'd probably forgotten he had it. McCabe's list of crimes include rustling and bank robbery.'

'No stages? Cricklewood must have converted him. Charlie Priest argued that stages were the easier target.'

'But we still ain't sure of the place,' Mason said.

Ben fingered his hat, pressing the brim into shape. 'Weren't there a mention on Cricklewood's dodger about him sometimes using explosives to block a stage road?'

'Then that suggests Sunstroke,' Davison advised. 'The road cuts through a low ravine.'

Ben glanced at Garner. 'Would you favour Sunstroke?'

The depot manager was looking worried. 'I'm concerned about explosives. What about that recent dynamite theft from Fred Venner's hut?'

Nobody spoke, then Mason said: 'Charlie was dealing with it. He'd said nothing further ... So, is that all?'

Jensen raised a hand. 'Chances are, this robbery'll be at Sunstroke Rocks; so we ought to draft a letter for Ben to present to the Sparville sheriff in case he needs assistance.'

'Then while you're sorting that out,' Ben said, 'how about someone giving me a conducted tour of Bleak Springs?'

'My pleasure,' Mason volunteered. 'It shouldn't take long.'

Straddling leather, Clipper faced the weak warmth of the sun. The morning's activity had made a slow start. Now, after a pervading fragrance of woodsmoke, bacon and coffee, men were waiting word to move out. But Clipper felt like he could never mount up again.

'Clipper!'

The voice sliced through his woozy thoughts. McCabe stalked over, swinging his quirt.

'You scatty bastard. You're supposed to be driving the wagon, not trying to break your fool neck on a horse.'

Clipper made a burbling sound. 'Wagon ...?' He clung to the saddle horn. 'That doc told me to rest.'

'You just been resting.' McCabe's eyes sparkled with irritation. 'And you're supposed to be looking after Renny.'

'Renny? ... Oh, yeah – where's Renny?'

'Goddammit. On the wagon. Are you driving him or not? You can handle a two-horse team, can't you?'

How could he have forgotten Renny?

'Damned cripples.' McCabe exhaled his frustration.

Clipper cringed. 'I ain't no cripple.' He longed to be back on some hillside pasture. Sheep he could cope with; but these rough drifters ...

'Has Renny said anything during the night?'

Clipper made a surly face. 'Said anything? About what?'

McCabe fed him a long sceptical stare. 'I want to know the minute he shows signs of talking.' His eyes shrank to slits. 'And when you gonna take that damned bandage off your head?'

Clippers fingers dithered along the frayed linen.

'Curly needs a fresh mount. Give him yours.' McCabe strutted away to check the dousing of the fire.

Clipper slithered cautiously off the horse. He lurched towards the wagon and clambered up. He had to act capable.

Or McCabe might leave him with a bullet in his back.

# EIGHT

'What I don't figger,' Doc Mason said, leading Ben west behind the south-side buildings, 'is why they were so keen to keep Renny alive.'

'Yeah, me too.' Ben strode with conviction, scarcely aware of his former bruises. 'What's this about Fred Venner's dynamite theft? You reckon it's maybe linked with stopping a stage?'

'Hard to say.' Mason looked sombre. 'It happened a week back. But explosives and gold kinda go together.'

As they walked Mason pointed out some lesser features: disused lots, an abandoned signwriter's at the end. They crossed to the north side and trudged back along a shallow arroyo that ran behind the street. Stray hens from some coops were pecking around in it. Mason sidetracked towards an isolated building.

'You didn't know Bleak once had its own newspaper?'

'No,' said Ben, surprised. 'How long ago was that?'

'Ten or twelve years. This was the printing house.'

They peered in through a broken ground-floor window. Ben picked out machinery smothered in cobwebs and bird droppings. Beneath an overhead gallery a begrimed signboard, *BLEAK SPRINGS*

*CLARION*, lay amid chicken clawprints gathering dust.

'Editor arrived with his press hoping to drum life into the town. When the local seams failed, so did the paper. The editor took sick and died. His abandoned press is still here.'

Ben assessed the surroundings. The printing house faced a gap through which several south-side buildings could be seen: saloon, rooming house, some of the derelict lots.

'I expect you know the gunshop,' Mason said, moving on. 'I'll leave you to talk to Fred. It's almost surgery time.'

Fred Venner, the small sinewy gunsmith, greeted Ben wiping his oil-stained fingers on to his coarse apron.

'So you're the new marshal. What can I show you? I keep the guns well secured. Charlie Priest was keen on that.'

Ben took in the padlocked array of weapons. 'I ain't aimin' to increase my armoury just yet,' he drawled with a smile. 'I wanted to ask you about this dynamite theft.'

'That? Come out back. I'll show you the explosives hut.'

Venner led the way to a solitary log building near the east end of the ditch. 'Sonsofbitches smashed the hasps off. I got extra locks fitted now.' He opened up. Ben followed him in.

Venner tapped on a stack of boxes marked *DYNAMITE*. 'They took five boxes and two coils of fuse. During the night.'

'Did many folk know you kept it?'

Venner shrugged. 'It weren't a secret. They used a wagon. Charlie examined the tracks. He reckoned one of the left-side wheels had a flawed rim. It left V-shaped notches in the mud. On the day previous a farmer three miles out had a wagon and two-hoss team stolen. He reckoned the thieves wouldn't get far 'cause of a faulty wheel. Charlie wondered if this was the same wagon. You want to see what's left of the tracks?'

They moved out; Ben took a look. The V-marks were still there in places, despite being rained on and trampled.

Venner said: 'From the hoofprints, they headed west.'

'You keep a secure place anyway,' Ben said as Venner locked the hut again. 'You can sell me some gun-cleaning oil and a box of shells.'

Venner sorted out the purchases. 'Are you aiming to take up on that theft? 'Cause I just been talking with Davison. If my dynamite's gonna ambush a stage, it makes me feel responsible.'

'Don't matter where it came from,' Ben reassured him, 'it all blows up the same. It's where it can be used I got to think of next.'

Ben was sorting out his saddlebags at the livery when hooves came clopping up outside.

'Howdy, Ben.' Colly met him with a cheery smile.

'Colly,' he greeted her. 'I heard you'd gone visiting.'

'Yes, had to tell the folks about Grandpa being shot.'

She looked refreshed, keen to face the day. She was wearing a darker range rig: split riding skirt with buckskin fringes and a thick jacket to combat the chill. She handed the reins to Jimmy, saying she'd pick the mare up later. Ben wondered if she had seen Frank anywhere, but decided not to mention it.

Colly eyed his badge. 'I hear I missed an eventful night.'

'We could have done without it.' Ben gave a saddened grin. 'It brought me a new status. I'm heading for Sparville shortly to consult the sheriff. There's a hold-up brewing.'

'You can tell me in your office in an hour. I'm going to collect a few provisions.'

Ben went for a meal then sat down in the chilly office to think. It felt strange to be occupying a dead man's chair. He checked his .45. Satisfied, he tilted his hat back with the muzzle while he considered the issues concerning him, such as the whereabouts of McCabe. Was he behind the dynamite theft?

Ben was just wondering how to tell Colly about Frank when she walked in and took a seat by the cold stove.

'No fire? There's kindling in the corner.'

'Ain't worth it.' Ben found himself admiring the dark curls nestling between her hatbrim and the cream bandana. Sunlight filtering through the window tinted her complexion.

'So where's this hold-up gonna be?' she asked.

'Maybe Sunstroke Rocks. I'll look it over on my way to Sparville.' Ben told her more of the saloon shootout and the notes found on the gunslinger. 'McCabe and Cricklewood had been due to join forces.'

Colly sighed. 'And I still ain't found Galliard. Did you learn if your brother had been to the Rocking Y?'

Ben hedged. 'Colly, there's something I gotta explain –'

'When I came through Bleak three days back,' she went on, unheeding. 'I had a word with Marshal Priest; but no luck.' Her voice gathered sudden strength. 'Ben, I'd like you to go after this man Galliard.'

'What?' Ben stared in surprise. 'Hey, steady on, Colly –'

'It was your idea I seek Priest's help. Well, you're

behind the badge now. Or – you ain't backing out already?'

'It ain't a question of backing out. What I said before was off the top of my head.'

A muscle puckered on her lip. 'Some head, marshal.'

'Look, I've the welfare of Bleak to consider –'

'You took Cricklewood. What's to stop you taking Galliard?'

Ben slammed a hand on to the desk. 'Cricklewood was mean-bad. When he shot Priest, I'd no choice.'

'No?' Her tone was sceptical; her eyes degraded him. 'Tale I heard, you hung back and let Priest move in first –'

'Colly, if you were ten years younger I'd spank you for that.' On his feet, Ben stood over her. He caught the relenting flash in her eye and strode to the window to contain himself. 'The man you're chasing ain't a bit like Cricklewood.' Turning, he sat down on a corner of the desk. 'There were four players in that poker game. Two got drilled, one escaped. The fourth man happened to be my brother.'

A mystified frown rucked her brow. 'The brother you've been searching for?'

'Brother Frank, none other. I thought by now you might have learned my second name. It's Galliard. And the Galliard you're chasing is Frank Galliard, my brother.'

Colly had started to rise. She sank down again slowly. 'Then why in tarnation didn't you tell me?'

'I been trying to, but ...' Ben lapsed into a shrug. 'When you first said you were hunting a Galliard it gave me a jolt. But Frank's explained, your Grandpa dying was an accident –'

'You think I don't know his story?' she shrilled. She rose pacing, eyes ablaze as she slapped at the fringes of her jacket. 'You make me feel a right fool. Where is he now?'

'How the hell do I know. He rode out early.' Ben paused, a glint of his humour breaking through. 'Colly, this is crazy. Both of us seeking the same man and meeting like we did. A million to one, I'd reckon, but Frank ain't a killer.'

Colly took a sobering breath. 'Reckon on this, mister hot-shot marshal. Your brother could have changed.'

Ben fell silent. Priest had made a similar point.

'So when are you starting out for Sparville?' she asked.

Ben pulled his thoughts into line. 'When I've picked up the council's letter. I'm just wondering if Frank's gone there.'

'To give himself up?'

'To convince the sheriff he's innocent.'

'Some hope. He could have lit out to save you embarrassment of arresting your own brother ... Well, I've been doing some thinking.' Her tone took on a bitter-sweet edge. 'Maybe I'll ride to Sparville with you. I've got good reason.'

Ben shrugged. 'No objection.' Let the girl stew on her problems, he decided. Even if they set out at loggerheads, by the time they arrived he might have got her views converted.

'I'll tell the council,' he confirmed. 'If I'm found with a slug in my back they'll know who to look for.'

'I only shoot marshals in the chest,' she said tartly.

'Like mountain lions? If we meet any of those you'd best leave the shooting to me.'

Clipper clung to the seat, wondering if the rickety wheel would last. His struggles to prevent the wagon from veering were making his bandaged brow itch with sweat. It wasn't the cargo of dynamite he was fretting over. He wanted to give Renny a comfortable ride.

Snatches of talk drifted in from the riders.

'Slim would have needed some persuading,' McCabe was telling Chub. 'He was too set in his ways.'

'You done much lootin' with him?' Chub asked.

'Some. We weren't the best of company.' McCabe sounded broody. 'Last time we met we argued about Sunstroke Rocks. But now I don't have to convince him any more.'

'Even so, you lost two marksmen. And Curly's still nursing a finger. Did Curly tell you the fourth poker player was brother to that deputy who drilled Slim?'

'The hell he was. I don't see that affecting anything.'

Chub called across to the wagon: 'Hey, Clipper – is Renny makin' speeches yet?'

Startled, Clipper flinched. 'Wha-at? ... No, he's – no.' Renny had only moaned on and off.

Chub flicked his cigarette away. 'You been dreaming this job up a long time, McCabe. What if Renny don't recover?'

McCabe grew vindictive. 'If Renny's tolling his knell, we'll go ahead anyway. We've enough dynamite. But it would be easier if he could talk.' He nudged the claybank ahead.

Clipper sifted through the conversation. It meant little.

The front wheel wobbled; the wagon clattered.

Renny was starting to moan again.

# NINE

Ben bought supplies, paid his debts at the rooming house, collected his Springfield and picked up the roan. When he called at Davison's for his introductory letter, Doc Mason was leaning on the counter talking to the clothier.

'That night you were taken to Blackfoot Bluff,' Ben asked him, 'did you hear anyone talking of dynamite?'

Mason shook his head. 'Come to think though, there were some boxes of something on the wagon with Renny.'

'Maybe that was it. They'd no wagon when I ran into 'em, but it could have been at Blackfoot already.'

At the clop of hooves Ben glanced out to find Colly waiting. A glint in her eyes revealed an impatience to get started.

'Good day, Miss Wells,' Mason called. 'I hope you'll look after our marshal in Sparville. We need him in one piece.'

'I'll watch him,' she responded. 'But no guarantees.'

Ben handed the office keys to Mason, bade the two men goodbye, and mounted his roan.

For a while they rode in silence, holding a steady lope. The sky remained azure bright, the air keen and brisk.

They passed Buffalo Skulls. As Colly turned

right for the uphill track Ben continued straight on.

'What's the idea sticking to the stage road?' she called. 'What's wrong with the track up by the timber?'

Ben reined in and faced her patiently. 'It may cut out the bend but it ain't a trail to take a wagon up. Satisfied?'

Glaring, she jerked her heels at the mare's flanks. 'Strikes me this marshal's job is going to your head.' Smouldering inwardly, she continued after him.

The road was good and wide, sticky in patches with a meltwater softness. Wheeltracks and hoofprints intermingled.

Ben tried for small talk. 'How well d'you know Doc Mason?'

Colly shrugged. 'He visits the homestead. He's reliable.'

'He took me on a tour of the town.' Ben added details of the dynamite theft. 'Will you recognise Sunstroke Rocks when we reach it?'

'Sure. It's hard to miss, 'specially at sundown.'

He felt pleased that she was conversing again.

Presently Colly's curiosity showed. 'Why d'you keep glancing down at the roadside?' she asked. 'You practising sign-reading?'

'You could say that.'

She twisted full-face towards him. 'Are you keepin' tight-mouthed for the whole trip, marshal? If I knew what you were looking for, I might even help.'

Ben relented. 'I'm looking for a left-side track with a V-notch in the wheel rim. It could be the wagon used to shift the dynamite.'

She viewed him with disbelief. 'Ain't that a long shot?'

'Sure. It's as chancy as calling a stacked deck. But

there ain't been much rain and it's no trouble to check on. The wagon might even have turned off for Blackfoot Bluff.'

'You ain't striking off that way surely? It's off route.'

'No. I'm assuming McCabe's party brought it back on to the road after disposing of the cattle.'

They continued until Colly halted the mare.

'You don't mind me asking' – her tone touched on cynicism – 'but do rustlers make a point of robbing stages?'

Ben slowed the roan. 'You should be asking, do hold-up men make a point of rustling. Some might. I reckon most of those villains had dabbled in other things. One was a failed sheepman. Clipper. I spoke with him; he seemed to regret the company he kept. If I'd been him, I'd have regretted keeping sheep.'

'You don't go much for sheep, do you?' Colly steadied the mare, maintaining a faint air of defiance. 'The world ain't all cows. If you lived on a homestead you might realise this.'

Ticked off, Ben rummaged for his Bull Durham and began to roll a smoke. He struck a match on the pommel and lit up.

'How many villains are in this bunch?' she asked.

'At least nine. Two could be hamstrung: Renny and Clipper. Others might have met up, including Curly who hightailed from the Blue Norther. A biggish party.' He rowelled the flanks of the roan. 'Let's move.'

He rode thoughtfully until they took a slight incline. Suddenly he drew rein, swung down, and crushed out his smoke.

'Take a look at this.' He indicated the tracks.

Colly dismounted and sank down beside him.

'We've found ourselves a muddy stretch.' Ben pointed. 'And one wagon track with a V-notch gash on the wheel rim.'

Colly glanced around. 'There's another impression here. And more further along. They're about nine feet apart.'

'Yeah.' Ben tipped back his hat. 'It sure looks like they headed that dynamite wagon towards Sunstroke Rocks.'

They pushed onwards. Population was thin in this region of Montana. They passed only an occasional horseman and waved to an eastbound stage. They met a trio of ditty-chanting miners with shovels cinched to their burros.

'How's prospectin'?' Ben greeted them.

'Dying,' one replied. 'Not like five years back.'

Ben wondered. If less gold was coming out of Sparville, how might this affect any plan of McCabe's to rob a stage?

'There's a good watering place about five miles on,' Colly said a while later, leaning forward to pat Belle's neck. Ben realised the friction between them had subsided.

They reached the watering place, a roadside stream. Ben surveyed it. 'It ain't that easy for a hoss to reach.'

Dismounting, he scrambled down and scooped up a hatful of water for the roan to drink. He was fetching a second hatful for Colly's mare when he slithered down on one knee. 'Durn it!' He heard Colly's laugh from further upstream.

'If you'd come along here your hoss could have got down.' She already had the mare drinking from the shallows.

Ben dashed water from his pants leg. 'Well, it weren't as bad as the last drenching I took,' he grinned, recalling how Chub had hauled him through the stream and fire.

They ate some of Colly's sourdough biscuits then resumed riding. When the timber track emerged on their right, Colly said: 'We're about twenty miles from Sparville.'

'Five more, then I reckon we'll make camp.'

The light was shrinking as they moved off the road and off-saddled. Ben heaped a small fire together. As Colly prepared food – flapjacks, Ben's bacon and chilli, and more of her biscuits – Ben kept the blaze crackling with twigs and pine needles while holding his damp leg towards it.

The fireglow flickered over Colly's features, emphasizing her eyes. She could make someone a good steady partner, he decided, if only she would relax her crusade.

She darted a sharp glance at him. 'Why you so tense? Ain't you seen a woman cook before?'

Ben felt himself colouring. 'I guess I was just wondering how this is all gonna turn out.' He lobbed another twig into the embers. 'D'you honestly believe Frank is guilty?'

She seemed to hesitate. 'I ain't had cause to change views.'

Ben left it at that. When they positioned their bedrolls, he saw no sign of any Derringer being sneaked amid her blankets.

'Strange name you've got,' she murmured. 'Galliard. It's a dance. Did you know? Seems ages since I were at a dance.'

After a pause he said: 'I never was much good even with the fiddles scraping. There ain't been chance lately.'

Brooding on his past and future Ben fell asleep.

They washed in a tiny stream, icy enough to make Ben glad to grab his towel. He watched Colly tie her hair back. 'You're made of sterner stuff than me.' She rewarded him with a smile.

They struck camp after breakfast in the metallic dawn light. A morning for easy riding and sober thinking.

Presently Colly pointed ahead to a narrow defile which lay between short cliffs. 'We're almost at Sunstroke Rocks.' Ben approached it slowly, studying it.

'Can't be above fifty feet high.'

They halted in the defile. Ben scanned the jagged overhang. He stood in his stirrups, peering ahead, then twisted in the saddle. 'Good for a hold-up, d'you think?'

Colly shrugged. 'You tell me. I'm no expert.'

'As the stage rolls in, block the far end with a rockfall. Let's take a look up that dry gully.'

They left the horses cropping grass while they clambered up. Ben reached out a hand to help Colly up the final stretch. As they peered back down, Ben began to roll himself a smoke.

'They'd only need to use a few sticks of dynamite.'

He eyed the land from the foothill country to the higher forest. He gestured into the defile where the rock buttresses were streaked with crimson and sepia.

'Is that how the place got its name?'

'I believe so. With good clouds at sundown, everything gets tinted a vivid red. As though the sun was painting it.'

'You got a dainty way of putting things.' Smoke trickled from Ben, drifting on the still air. 'You sound like an artist.'

'Maybe that's what led me west. Soakin' up the magic.' Her eyes brightened and she blinked her memories away.

Ben trod his smoke out. 'Let's go back down.'

For an hour they kept a firm pace. The grassland became broken with scrub oak and pine. Ben paused frequently to scan the terrain. He noticed Colly observing him.

'Just like to keep my eyes peeled,' he said.

Twice he walked his roan off the road to examine the remains of old campfires. Colly began to look bored. He grinned at her. 'We'll still be in Sparville by mid-afternoon.'

After a third detour they were returning to the road behind a shelf of rock when he spotted a campfire patch nearby. 'That looks recent. It ain't so puddled.' Halting the roan, Ben glanced about. 'I'd say a biggish party camped here.'

He was about to lead on when Colly called: 'Ben, look.'

His gaze followed her finger pointing to marshy wheel tracks. There was a V-notch shape in the mud.

'Colly, you'll make a sign-reader yet.' He jumped down with a grin of pleasure. The tracks were quite clear. 'Notice that wobbly wheel?' Leading the roan, he began to follow them downslope. 'Who'd want to bring an unsafe wagon off the road?'

The tracks entered a draw on the right. Ben signalled for caution till he was certain there was no one around. Jammed into the bushes was a wagon with a rumpled tarpaulin on its bed. Reaching, he jerked the tarp aside.

'Five boxes of dynamite,' he said. 'Looks like they hid the wagon when the wheel started playing tricks then took off with the team.' He eased up a split-open lid. 'This one's half empty.' He tested the weights of the other boxes. 'The rest seem full.'

'But they'd hardly abandon four and a half boxes,' Colly said.

'No. They could be back with another wagon. They probably took the missing sticks with them.' Ben stooped to examine the rickety front wheel. 'And here's the V-gash on the rim.'

He began to notice other items. 'Someone left his hat.' He indicated a fancy braided tan stetson. 'Blankets, a pair of worn boots. Another tarp used as a mattress.'

Ben wiped his face. In the shelter of the draw the motionless air captured a touch of noon heat. A few bluetails were buzzing noisily.

Colly stood chewing a corner of her lip. 'Ben, why've they brought the wagon so far past Sunstroke Rocks?'

'Dunno.' He shook his head, puzzled. 'It bothers me.' He flicked a fly from the back of his hand and began to circuit the wagon. Some of the scrub looked badly trampled.

Again he swiped away a fly. 'Damn bluetails starting an early season ...' He broke off as several more flies rose in a buzzing swarm.

'What is it, Ben?' He heard Colly start forward and he raised a restraining hand.

'Don't come too close. We got ourselves a corpse.'

# TEN

The dead man lay belly down amid tangled grass, head twisted sideways. Insects were walking through his beard and between his lips. Congealed blood fouled his lank hair.

Colly hesitated, but only briefly. 'I ain't squeamish.' She drew alongside Ben as he sank to his haunches.

'Shot in the head. Looks like he was dragged off the wagon.' Ben peered at a dark stain over the left shoulder blade. Crouching lower, he eased the body up a shade.

Colly said: 'Shot in the back too?'

'Nope. In the chest, some time ago. The wound's been dressed once but started bleeding again.' Ben straightened up. 'I reckon this is Renny. I remember that fancy hat; and I'm the one who gave him that first bullet.' His lips tightened. 'Hell and doggone it. If I'd dropped him dead in the first place it would have saved a helluva lot of trouble.'

'So why's he been shot again now?'

'Maybe McCabe got the information he was seeking.'

Ben gingerly checked the pockets but found little of value.

Colly pointed to a scrap of trampled paper. 'What's this?'

Ben picked it up. 'Looks like a withdrawal slip

from the Sparville bank.' A few numbers were scrawled on the back.

Ben stuffed the slip into his pocket, spread a tarpaulin over the dead man and weighted the edges with stones.

'We'll notify the sheriff at Sparville.'

Sitting a spare horse from the team, Clipper clung grimly to its mane. He wiped a knuckle at his runny nose.

'That's the nearest you'll get to a saddle horse,' they had warned him. 'Topple off, and you're as good as dead.'

And only an hour ago, McCabe had raged: 'Why didn't you watch the damned wheel? You were in charge of the wagon.'

Clipper caught the droning voice of Chub: 'What are we doing about a replacement, McCabe?'

'Someone can look for one as we pass the farms. Take it back to the draw and pick up the rest of the dynamite.'

What Clipper didn't figger was why Lou and Pierre had been sent on ahead to Sparville. Hadn't someone said they'd gone looking for a wagon as well? He wished he wasn't so confused. Brainwork gave him a headache.

More and more he felt he was living on borrowed time.

Back on the stage road Ben studied the hoofprints. 'They're making for Sparville. No doubt on that.'

Colly asked: 'What d'you think McCabe was hoping to learn from Renny?'

'I'd give more than a dollar to know.'

They began to pass a farm or two and soon they were gazing on the smoke haze of Sparville. Its buildings were tall and solid. Spiderlegs of streets sprawled from a central roadway.

'First good-sized burg I've seen in a while,' Ben said.

As they made their way down, Colly pulled ahead. She sat the mare well; fine-shaped, attractive. This past day their differences had melted in companionship. But now Ben sensed a nagging disquiet that such moments were about to dwindle.

Clipper kept his distance as McCabe halted the riders and pointed his quirt towards Sparville.

'You're looking down on a fortune, you know that?'

His meaning was lost on Clipper.

McCabe fixed his chill slate eyes on the men. 'Make this a quiet ride in. Two of you bring Clipper through the main street with me. The rest – small groups only. Just get the lie of the place.'

'Where are we meeting up?' Chub asked.

'North edge, by the horsetrader's corral. Lou and Pierre should be waiting. They should have found a wagon by now.'

Wagontalk, wagontalk ... Clipper pressed a hand to his thudding temples. The bandage was hanging in near tatters.

Hadn't three men stopped by a farm to root out a wagon? Nat and Lance – McCabe's lookouts; and the blotchy Owen. So why this other wagon sought by Lou and Pierre?

Clipper abandoned the riddle to reflect on Renny. At the draw Renny had roused. McCabe had pressed him for information, but cast aside the scrap of paper Renny had produced. All he had wanted was a name. Clipper couldn't recall whose.

He just felt a sad sort of relief not to be caring for a sick pard any more. But he hadn't liked watching McCabe finish him off.

Not least of the questions nagging at Ben was his

brother. Was Frank now back in Sparville? He drew the roan alongside Colly's mare. 'Did you and Frank ever talk much?' he asked.

Colly's expression was hard to read. 'We talked – briefly, before his arrest. It wasn't very pleasant. I mean, would you enjoy arguing with a man who's supposed to have shot your Grandpa?'

'You say "supposed to". Are you having doubts? Would the sheriff have encouraged you to trail Frank if he was dangerous?'

'Quayle was as angry as hell when your brother broke jail.'

'Yeah, I guess I'd have been too. Heat of the moment.'

'Well, I hope you're ready to face him,' Colly said tartly. 'He'll probably think you're trying to take over his job.'

She fell silent, then in an outburst of uncertainty confessed: 'I just don't know what to make of your brother. I really only went after him to talk some more.' She threw a sharp glance at Ben. 'I still ain't had proper chance.'

'So you think he'll be back in Sparville?'

'Frank ain't my reason for coming back. Nor are you.'

She gave a twitch at the reins and drew ahead again.

Clipper sagged against a stringer of the horsetrader's corral. That canter along Sparville's Main Street had bushed him worse than curbing a prize ram on heat.

Every few minutes some of the men would chortle as McCabe regaled them with another story of his escapades. Clipper was sick of McCabe's boasting to this hero-worshipping rabble.

He was sick of himself.

'So, we're all here apart from our dynamite trio.'

McCabe ceased his bragging and scanned his followers. 'Pierre, you had no problem finding a wagon? Where've you hidden it?'

'Middle of town.' The gingery French-Canadian grinned. 'Lou picked out a secluded yard behind the billiard hall.'

Satisfied, McCabe reached a decision. 'Curly, you know Sparville? Then ride back in with me. I got a few matters to fix. The rest of you, get some grub into you. Stay inconspicuous. I ain't sure yet when we'll move. Could be hours, or even a day or two.'

As McCabe walked towards his claybank, he paused beside Clipper. 'Ain't you taken that goddam rag off your skull yet?'

Clipper flinched. Removing his coonskin hat he started to coax the bandage from his brow.

'If that's how you mollycoddle your woollybacks ...' McCabe grabbed at the dressing and wrenched it free. Clipper yelped.

McCabe gave the healing wound a cursory glance. 'You'll live.' He mounted the claybank to accompany Curly back into town.

The men were sniggering. Clipper dabbed at his forehead and examined his reddened fingertips. He dragged the coonskin back on, low down to hide the seepage of blood.

# ELEVEN

Ben and Colly rode into Sparville past the first buildings: Fergus's, the wagoner's shop; the Grubstake cafe; and across from it the smart-looking Elkhorn hotel.

'We could do worse than stay there,' Ben drawled. 'But business first.' Then, he thought, a welcome meal.

'Quayle's office is in the centre of Main,' Colly said.

Ben appraised the busy sidewalks. Nearing a stretch of prominent brownstone, he said: 'Ease up, Colly.' He paused while a buckboard clattered by. 'I could have sworn I glimpsed McCabe coming out of that brownstone with a younger man.'

Colly glanced across. 'They ain't there now.'

'They turned up that street. The younger one reminded me of that fourth at poker, Curly. But I'd best avoid a confrontation until I've talked with Quayle.'

They left their horses at the livery. Quayle's office lay beyond the brownstones, a trim building with a clapboard front.

'You'd best leave this to me,' Ben said.

'Suits me. I'd prefer to talk with Quayle alone.'

Sheriff Quayle, a scrawny man with cadaverous eyes, was polishing his boots with harness wax as they walked in. The tarnished star on his vest matched the square of office carpet. His eyes chilled over as he saw Colly.

Ben introduced himself. 'I'm just in from Bleak Springs.' He presented his letter.

Quayle scanned it. 'Newly appointed marshal? Word reached me about Priest. Are you the one who drilled Cricklewood?'

Ben nodded. Quayle studied the letter some more while Colly took a seat by the wall. Ben tucked a thumb into his belt.

'Seems in order,' the sheriff summed. He glanced at Colly. 'Cornelia Wells. So what brings you back?'

'We rode in together,' Ben said.

'I ain't asking you; I'm asking her. Did you catch up with that jail-buster Galliard?'

'You'd best deal with the Bleak Springs marshal first.'

'Why? Who gave him priority? Hey, whoah on ... Galliard?' Quayle snatched for Ben's letter again.

'Frank Galliard's my brother.'

'The hell he is. Is that why you're here?'

'I'm here to forestall a stage robbery. A bunch of jaspers led by a rider called McCabe could already be here in town.'

Quayle deliberated, and screwed the lid on to his tin of wax. Ben could sense his underlying resentment.

'So what do you want to know?'

'Gold schedules, stage movements. What check d'you keep?'

'Stage times are on that notice-board. Gold schedules ... To run 'em regular would be tempting fate.'

Ben gestured at the notice-board. 'You got a rogue's gallery here. McCabe could still be gathering men. I've tangled with him once already.' Ben gave an account. 'But now he's going on to richer pickings.'

Quayle leered. 'What's he look like?' He turned to his display of dodgers.

'Tall, straw-headed. Rides a claybank. His picture ain't up there.' Ben added details of the ride from Bleak.

The sheriff rasped a hand around his chin. 'Sounds like Tepee Creek where you found Renny's body. But if you think this hold-up's gonna be at Sunstroke Rocks, why'd they bring the dynamite that far? Tepee's this side of Sunstroke.'

'Ain't sure.' A new thought nudged at Ben. 'How secure are places in Sparville? The assay office, for instance.'

Quayle cast him a scornful glance. 'Nobody's gonna steal from there. The place for a raid's out in the open. If McCabe's in town he could be seeking knowledge on wagon movements.'

Ben began to pace, his bootheels deadened by the carpet. 'Would the assay know the gold shipments leaving the mines?'

'Why should they?' Quayle produced an unfriendly scowl. 'You're asking a helluva lot of questions.'

'I'm trying to find a starting point.'

'Then why don't you visit the assay?' Quayle wound up grittily. 'Sure, they keep a fair-sized safe, but it's protected. Pineboard and brownstone building, north end of town.'

'I could show him,' Colly offered.

Quayle shifted his gaze towards her. 'Ain't you and me got some talking of our own to catch up with, Miss Wells?'

'Whenever you're ready,' Colly acquiesced.

With a feeling that Quayle was shucking his responsibility, Ben delivered a bogus smile. 'I'd hate to listen in on you.' He snatched back his letter. 'I'll drop by again later.'

Clipper sat awhile by the corral rail, trying to sift the

conversation. McCabe, back from town again with Curly, seemed to be advising caution.

Chub expressed disbelief. 'You're sure it was him?'

'More than sure.' McCabe surveyed his cohorts. 'He was near the bank, riding in with a woman. Full marshal's badge. What's more, Curly tells me he's the one who shot Slim.'

'You reckon he's gonna cause trouble?' asked Chub.

'Why should he? He doesn't know anything.'

'Then what's he doing in Sparville?'

McCabe sighed tetchily. 'Tell 'em about the brother, Curly.'

'I only know what the brother told Slim when he joined us at poker. He'd just busted out of the Sparville jail.'

'So more'n likely,' McCabe said, 'this marshal's here to sort out the mess his brother's in. We don't need to worry.'

Chub went on: 'Did you find our contact man in town?'

'Yeah. I'm calling back when it's more convenient to talk.' McCabe glanced about, concerned. 'Lance and Owen not back yet?'

'Nope. You reckon they've picked another dud wagon?'

McCabe grimaced, saying nothing.

A knot of cramp gripped Clipper in the leg; yet he felt one flicker of comfort. He was starting to grasp McCabe's plan.

Ben slammed the assay door and stalked fuming down Main Street past Quayle's office. His indignation only fizzled out as a rail-hitched horse caught his eye. Approaching cautiously, he noted a partly healed score mark on the critter's yellow rump, and recalled how McCabe's horse had shied from the sting of a bullet. But there was no sign of McCabe now.

A stage came clattering in to halt outside one of the brownstones. Two muscle men in derby hats were riding double shotgun. From the building two soberly garbed gents emerged dragging a trolley. Boxes were swiftly unloaded from stage to trolley, and trundled inside. Only now did Ben realise that this edifice was the Sparville bank.

Curious, he sauntered round the back. Russet Street, which ran behind the bank was deserted, apart from some roof workers up a ladder on the far side. Now that his temper was cooling, Ben decided to go back and consult Quayle.

The sheriff was sitting alone, writing with a scratchy pen. He glanced up. 'Find anything at the assay office?'

'No. Did you expect me to?' The feeling that Quayle was using him persisted. 'What have you done with Colly Wells?'

'She went for a meal, and maybe to book in at the Elkhorn.'

'Well, I've just seen McCabe's claybank. I know it's his from a bullet graze on the rump.'

Mystified, Quayle tossed his pen down. 'So?'

'Aw, come on, Quayle. You sent me to the assay chasing tumbleweed. You didn't expect 'em to help. You're in closer touch with gold movements than they are.'

'Is that what they told you? Now see here' – Quayle slammed a palm on to his desk – 'one Galliard for me's been enough. I don't need you stirring trouble.'

Ben took a turn around the carpet. 'Look, I know you don't like me invading you; but if we're to stop these buzzards we oughta work together. Right?' Ben waited for Quayle's sullen nod. 'Then chew on the assay's only suggestion. The robbery may not be for gold leaving Sparville, but for money coming in.'

Quayle meditated. 'But folk still barter in nuggets –'

'Quayle, you're up in tentville. I just seen a stage off-loading into the bank. Extra guard. Big money –'

'Are you plumb out of your goddam mind? The bank's a less likely target than the assay. The strongroom's the toughest to reach the west, with the latest in time locks. Laycock's assured me, and he's been manager for years. Forget it.'

'I'm talking about money before it arrives, coming through Sunstroke Rocks. When's the next big shipment due in?'

'Not for some days if one's just arrived.'

'Which gives McCabe time to prepare. I saw him earlier near the bank. He could have been checking on incoming deliveries.'

'And you imagine the bank'd tell him?' Quayle stood up, glowering. 'Let's get one thing straight, Galliard. This is a respectable town. Sure, there's cathouses. Miners get liquored. But the only recent killing was that incident in the timber, with your brother. Until today, even petty pilfering's declined.'

'So what happened today?'

'Some carpetbags vanished from a store.' Quayle began to preen his fingernails. 'And a coupla wagons went missing.'

'Wagons? Ben braced a little, more alert. 'Where from?'

'One disappeared from the yard at Wright's sawmill, early before the town was stirring. Why?'

'Just thinking about that dynamite again.'

'They'd hardly lift a town wagon for that.'

'What about the second one?'

'Well, maybe ... I sent two men to Tepee Creek.

They just rode in. Found Renny's body, like you said; but no dynamite. Coming back, they met Truscott, a farmer. He was complaining he'd had a newly painted wagon stolen. Those jaspers could have taken it to the draw.'

'But wouldn't Colly and me have passed 'em?'

'They could have been up some sodbuster's cart-track.'

Ben mulled this over then asked: 'You've never had any problems at the bank?'

The sheriff considered. 'Once, two years gone. A light-fingered teller took off with some money.' Frowning, he turned to sift through a wad of papers. He paused at one of the sheets. 'Yeah, I thought the name clicked. The teller was called Renny. Says here he could have become a drifter.'

Ben fished into his pocket. 'This kinda confirms it. We found it near his body. A Sparville bank payment slip.'

Quayle perused it. 'What are these numbers written on it?'

'Dunno. Schedules for the big deliveries maybe?'

'These hardly look like times and dates.' The sheriff grimaced. 'Are you saying McCabe got this from Renny then chucked it away? Why do that?'

'Out of date? So McCabe visited the bank to check.'

Quayle scratched his jowl. 'There was talk of another clerk, Bryceman, being in cahoots with Renny. He's still at the bank.'

'Then maybe Renny supplied McCabe with Bryceman's name before he was shot. But we'll need to know ourselves when the next big delivery's due if we're to protect it. Can't you check with this manager man, Laycock?'

'I could if I was convinced.' Quayle shifted moodily.

Ben snorted. 'Quayle, ain't you gonna do a

damned thing?'

'Now that ain't fair. I already told you I sent deputies to Tepee. Well, one of 'em saw your brother ride in this morning. Cornelia Wells don't know about it yet.'

'Frank — back in Sparville?' Ben straightened up.

'Yeah. And the girl's starting to change her thinking.'

'On Frank?' Ben stared at him. 'What's convinced her?'

'You. Or even me. 'Cause I ain't got the fixation folk assume 'bout his guilt. My bleat's against him busting jail.'

Ben masked a grin. 'Only 'cause he ain't guilty.'

'That's your opinion.' Quayle met him with unkind eyes. 'So if he's here to square with me, why ain't he appeared yet?'

'Maybe he's finding it hard to face. Quayle, are you gonna stir your skinny butt and show some interest in this robbery?'

'But we still ain't sure when — hey, where you going?'

Ben swung for the door with a slap at his holster. 'Place I was going when I saw the claybank. To check that McCabe ain't hired a wagon.'

The sign above the gateway said '*G. FERGUS – WAGON HIRE.*' Ben ambled into a yard cluttered with buckboards. He found the grizzled wagonman squatting beside a cart. A fair-headed youth was helping him to repair an axle.

'Mr. Fergus?' Ben introduced himself. 'Have any strangers been in about hiring a wagon during the last day or so?'

Fergus eyed Ben's badge. 'I get enquiries all the time.'

Ben pushed his hat back an inch. 'It's a long shot anyway. They pulled off the road near Tepee

Creek with a busted wheel. Thought I should check if they'd sought a replacement.'

'No-o ... Enquiries I get are mainly for buckboards, but from folk I know. Guess I can't help you, marshal.'

Ben nodded. 'Obliged anyway.' About to leave, he added: 'One of them's lean, straw-haired. I noticed his claybank tied out front a while back. It's missing now.'

'Lots of folk use that hitch-rail,' Fergus said.

The lad holding the axle glanced up. 'I saw that man leave his horse. I'd been to the store to get Mr Fergus some screws. And I'd seen him ride in earlier with three other men.'

'Three?' Ben wondered about the rest. 'Can you remember much about 'em? Big ears, busted noses, wooden legs?'

The youth grinned. 'They looked like they'd been riding awhile. One oldster in a coonskin hat looked real beat.'

Fergus glanced at Ben. 'If that's what Joe says he saw, you can bet it's right. He's an observant lad.'

Emboldened, Joe said: 'Ain't you gonna tell the marshal about Mr Wright? He was asking about a replacement.'

'Oh, yeah.' Fergus stirred, recollecting. 'He runs the sawmill. He reckoned he'd had a wagon stolen, around dawn.'

'And in the store today some customers were talking about farmer Truscott. He'd had his wagon taken this morning.'

'Truscott? He's just been painting it up.'

'That's worth knowing,' Ben said. He did not dampen Joe's pride by mentioning that he'd heard much of this from Quayle. 'Tell you what, Joe. If those riders do come in here, I'd be obliged if you'd say nothing about me asking questions.'

As Joe gave a cheery nod, Fergus said: 'Do I take

it these men are bad characters? Have you spoken to our sheriff?'

'Yeah, we had quite a session.' Ben broke off to find Joe staring at him with hero-worshipping eyes.

'Say, are you the marshal who shot Slim Cricklewood?'

'Who told you about that?' Ben asked, a shade embarrassed.

'One of the stage drivers. I had a cousin on a stage he held up five years ago. You wait till I tell him I met you.'

'Look, Joe. You'd do me a better favour by keeping it mum. And if Mr Fergus don't object — if you spot any of those men again, maybe you could let me know.' Ben dropped a ten-cents piece into Joe's palm. 'There's a second dime in it later.'

'He can start watching right away,' Fergus said. 'He's got to exchange those screws. They're the wrong pitch.'

Joe's eyes were shining as he stared at the coin. 'Thanks, marshal. Where'm I gonna find you?'

'Maybe the Elkhorn hotel.'

Fergus nodded his approval. 'Now you hear that good, Joe. This marshal's counting on you.'

Ben grinned. He followed Joe out through the yard, allowing him to hasten on ahead with the box of screws.

Two missing wagons ... But which one held the dynamite?

# TWELVE

After dozing awhile Clipper roused to find that Lance and Owen were back. McCabe was saying: 'Lance, we thought you'd picked another tumbledown wagon, you took that damned long.'

Owen chipped in: 'This one looks spanking new. We didn't waste time. Someone had been in the draw and found Renny.'

'So where's the dynamite now?'

'Granite Creek,' Lance said. 'Two miles north off the corduroy road. It's safe and handy. Nat's watching over it.'

As McCabe gave a grunt of approval, Clipper's eyes moistened. He didn't want to end up feeding the ants like Renny.

The men were always telling him to back off because he stank of sheep dirt. Well, maybe he'd back off now – for good.

With raucous breaths, Clipper fumbled alongside the stringers, afraid McCabe might be watching. But only a youth viewing horseflesh from the top rail kept glancing his way.

If only he knew where that marshal hombre was.

'Ignore him,' he heard McCabe say. 'He ain't going far.'

Wasn't he though? He could still ride to Granite Creek. Dynamite could hurt people, and it bothered Clipper.

As he hobbled from the corral corner to the

end-of-town tie-rack, he knew his thinking was askew. The mere notion of mounting up set his pulse thudding violently.

That kid on the stringer kept staring at him, but nobody else was taking much notice as Clipper reached his horse.

He felt the odds were at last moving in his favour.

Main Street was still busy. Ben crossed a sidestreet and stepped up on to the plankwalk, pondering his next move. Wherever McCabe and his villains might be, forestalling them without help from Quayle could be a thorny task.

Ben was signing the register at the Elkhorn hotel when Colly emerged from the lounge. 'Ben, you took your time.'

'Colly.' He led her back into the lounge. They sat side by side on a chintzy-frilled sofa. 'Did you manage to eat?'

'At the Grubstake cafe. You must try it.'

Ben told her of his wanderings: the assay office, the sheriff's, the wagoner's. 'McCabe's varmints can't be far away. Joe, the wagoner's help, has seen some of 'em already.' He sighed raggedly. 'Quayle says Renny used to work at the Sparville bank along with another shady clerk called Bryceman. McCabe might have been seeking Bryceman at the bank today to learn about the money intakes. I saw one lot arrive. It'll be a day or two before the next. That gives us breathing space.' He glanced at Colly. 'How did your own talk with Quayle go?'

She made a sour face. 'I ain't sure.'

'He told me you were changing your thinking.' Ben regarded her with a crooked smile. 'Does that let Frank off?'

Colly hesitated. 'It kinda looks as if Grandpa's death could have been accidental after all.'

Ben knew this remark must have cost her something in self-esteem. 'Quayle didn't tell you Frank's back in town.'

Her eyes widened. 'Is he? Come to think, I believe I glimpsed him going into the saloon. I wasn't sure what to do. I thought I should talk with you first.'

'Colly, I know it ain't easy for you, changing convictions. But I reckon the three of us should talk together.'

'I bin so concerned about Grandpa, I keep losing track.'

'We both do. Frank being here is a bonus. And then ...' He looked at her obliquely, reaping pleasure from her profile. 'I guess I got another reason. You, I mean –'

'Me?' In the shallow lighting of the lounge he thought he discerned a flush rising to her cheeks.

'Sure, why not? ... I guess I enjoy your company.' He grinned a little lamely. 'Talking with you and ...'

He leant towards her, nudging the soft cluster of hair nestling over her ear. 'Durn these brims,' he muttered. Snatching his hat off he reached for her, his mouth establishing contact on her cheek. As her breathing quickened he grew bolder, pressing his lips upon hers. She was warm, responsive with her tongue. Recovering, she eased him back though not in discouragement.

'Ben, remember where we are.'

'What the hell? Kissin' ain't a crime.' He grimaced in resignation. 'Trust me! Always choose the wrong moment –'

'Ben, I never meant that. Besides, you got a three-day trail stubble.' Mischievously she watched him finger his chin. 'If we're to talk with Frank, you'd better go find him.'

Collecting his wits, Ben pulled to his feet. 'Sit

tight while I check the saloon.' He was turning for a window view of the street when he suddenly jolted alert.

'What is it?' Colly caught his flash change of mood.

'Clipper.' Ben grabbed his hat. 'The sheep-shearing jasper's just shot past going hell for leather.'

By the time Ben had darted outside Clipper was spurting his horse beyond the end buildings. Ben turned back towards the hotel. Although the sheep-man had impressed him as the weak reed in McCabe's band, Ben was not sure what chasing him would achieve.

'Who's the cooncap ridin' licketysplit?'

Ben span round. 'Frank! I heard you were in town.' His brother was sauntering towards him, chewing on a dead match. 'I was just coming to drag you from the saloon.'

'I heard that rider thundering by.' Frank paused, frowning. 'Saloon? Is that the first place you look?'

'Colly Wells saw you go in. She's here in the hotel.'

'That so?' Frank grimaced. 'I think I seen that cooncap once before today, with some twenty odd mean-looking men.'

'Twenty? So McCabe's found extras. Where'd you spot 'em?'

'Near the horsetrader's corral. I was wandering there, straightening my thoughts. That Curly from the game – he was with 'em too.' Frank flicked the match into the mud and tapped a finger at Ben's star. 'Thought you'd quit; not taken promotion.'

'I'm here to obstruct McCabe. But come into the hotel. Colly's agreed, we should talk things out together.'

'Talk with her? Are you crazy?' Frank began to turn away.

'What the hell's wrong with talking?'

'You mean she don't want you to arrest me?'

'For God's sake, Frank, are you coming or not?'

Frank shrugged. 'I suppose I got little to lose.'

In the lounge Colly was standing by the window, hands clasped in composure. Ben knew this was an awkward moment for her.

Frank gave her an amiable nod. 'Howdy, Miss Wells. I hear we're gonna have a nice friendly threesome.'

Colly gestured towards a table and chairs in an alcove. 'Let's make ourselves comfortable, and hope we can agree.' They took seats. After a moment's silence, she said: 'Quayle seems ready to accept your story about Grandpa's death.'

"Bout time. But you're the one who's been dogging me.' Frank flickered a grimace towards her. 'If you're changing standpoint too. I'm mighty curious to know why.'

Colly hesitated. 'I bin brooding on it awhile.'

'So what about Hayley's version?' Frank asked. 'He saw me take the shotgun into the cabin.' He glanced at Ben. 'Old Eli sometimes fed me jack-rabbit supper, but he caught 'em in traps. I got the scattergun to convince him that were quicker. I left it propped inside his door while I visited his traps. Coming back, I saw Hayley. Didn't realise he'd just been in the cabin after hearing a gunshot. I waved, but he didn't wave back. He was riding for town.'

'To tell the sheriff Grandpa was dead,' said Colly.

Frank nodded glumly. 'Hayley said he'd found the shotgun resting on a crate. My first thought was, Hayley had shot him.'

'Hadn't you heard the shot yourself?' Ben asked.

'No. I was through the trees, beyond the higher ground.'

'But if you'd shot him, you'd hardly leave the shotgun behind.'

'My point all along. But there were three pouches of gold dust missing from a locker. Eli had been intending to stow 'em in a safer place. Hayley found the locker door open, but no gold. So did I; but when I reported the shooting to Quayle, Hayley was ahead of me. He argued I'd been hiding the gold in the trees when he saw me.'

'But why did Quayle pick on you to hold?' Ben asked.

'Why d'you think?' Frank retorted with venom. 'Quayle knew Hayley. I was the stranger.'

'So why's Quayle revising his ideas now?'

'Ain't we all revising 'em? I reckon that scattergun had slithered, hit the crate and jolted off. Quayle later took Hayley back to the cabin, looking for gold but they still didn't find any.' Frank glanced an apology at Colly.

As though this was her cue, she said: 'Not then. But Quayle told me today, after you busted out he went back again. Alone. This time he did find it, under the floorboards.'

Frank's mouth fell open. 'He did what?'

'Now you see why I'm changing standpoint. He noticed marks where a board had been prised up. He checked underneath.'

Frank gave a comical sigh. 'I can't deny I'm relieved. I remember noticing a few loose timbers by the door. Maybe your Grandpa shifted 'em to reach the floorboard. Then when he was shifting 'em back he knocked the shotgun and caught the full blast ... But I still don't figger how you guessed I'd head for Bleak Springs.'

'I was in Quayle's office once,' she said, 'when he took a meal along to your cell. I could hear you snarling about being better fed if you went back waddying near Bleak.'

'I changed my mind about waddying,' Frank grinned.

'Three bags of dust.' Ben looked at Colly. 'I suppose your folk'll inherit those.'

'Quayle's placing it in safe keeping. But I ain't tempting fate by saying where.' She gave a syrupy smile. 'It's the main reason I came back here. To ask Quayle if he'd found it.'

'Wa-all, I'm sure glad I ain't top target,' Frank drawled.

Ben summarized the recent ride from Bleak. 'Frank, did Cricklewood say anything of interest during that game, about teaming up with McCabe?'

'I scarcely noticed. Though Timbo vowed to make up his losses at Sunstroke Rocks if he didn't win the pot.'

'Sunstroke, eh?' Ben said, alerted. 'That confirms where the hold-up's to be. But I still ain't figgered why McCabe needs so many men. When you saw 'em, did Curly recognise you?'

'He just stared at me like I was a lodgepole pine.'

'And I'm still wondering about that cooncap.' Ben stood up and walked to the window. 'No one's ridden after him.'

Colly rose and sauntered over. 'D'you reckon Clipper was heading for Sunstroke?'

'Hardly, the state he's in. But I've a feeling if anyone's to leak more details of this robbery it could be him.'

Frank reached the window, planting his hands on the sill. 'Ben, if you're aiming to protect the stage you'll need assistance. And I don't mean Quayle. He could end up like a spooked heifer rather than bend to an outside marshal.'

'I've already told him, I ain't trying to run his office.'

'Yeah? I'm the one who should be offering you help.'

'It's not your concern, Frank.' Ben crooked a corner of his mouth. 'Your best bet is to square yourself with Quayle about busting jail. It might smooth his hackles about me interfering.'

'And make it soon,' Colly added. 'He knows you're here.'

Frank looked reluctant. 'You wouldn't want to come along, Ben?'

Ben considered. 'Not yet. I'm hoping he's checking on money intakes with the bank chief. Meanwhile, I'm gonna try the cafe.' He glanced at Colly. 'I'll see you here shortly, then I'll scout round for Clipper. I don't reckon he's able to ride far.'

The beef-steak Ben ate sitting in a Grubstake window seat was a cut above trail-side chilli and flapjacks. As he sluiced down the crumbs with coffee he noticed Joe coming out of the hotel. Ben rose and called from the doorway.

'Joe? You looking for me? Come and have a cup of java.'

When the lad was sitting opposite clutching a cup with eager hands, Ben asked: 'So? What have you come to tell me?'

'I saw one of those men ride out at a high lick.'

'Clipper, the one in the coonskin hat? Yeah, I saw him too. But no fret, Joe. What about the others? I heard some were grouping near a horsetrader's corral.'

Joe nodded. 'Yeah, I been listening to 'em talking.'

'The hell you have. What took you there?'

'I went to look at the horses after I'd exchanged those screws. The straw-haired man was there. Some of 'em were talking mean about the coonskin man till he sneaked off for his horse.'

'They would do. Clipper's an old woollyback-shearer. Could you hear what McCabe was saying –

the straw-haired man?'

'Some. After Clipper rode off someone asked, "What if he goes to the wagon?" McCabe said, "Nat can take care of him." Then he thought again and said to one called Chub, "You and Lance follow him, and warn Nat. Skirt round by the knoll."'

Ben pushed his cup aside. 'Did you hear any mention of dynamite? We think McCabe's planning to use some.'

'Dynamite?' Joe nodded, recollecting. 'Yeah, it could be on the wagon. They said it was at Granite Creek.'

'And how far's Granite Creek? And the knoll?'

'Coupla miles, east then north. It's easy to find. Follow the corduroy road. When it peters out, just keep going.'

Ben began to roll a smoke. 'Thanks, Joe. You done well. But don't go risking your neck, or I'll be in trouble with Mr Fergus. I hope you weren't too close to these men.'

'They took no notice of me.' Grinning, Joe suddenly looked enlightened. 'You reckon this is farmer Truscott's wagon? They said it looked spanking new and Truscott's was freshly painted.'

'It's as good a guess as any.'

Joe paused, eyes ashine. 'Marshal, what was it like shooting Slim Cricklewood? I sure wish I'd seen it.'

Ben wagged a stern finger. 'Now, Joe – I ain't done nothing marvellous. I'd have sooner had Marshal Priest alive.'

Ben paid for the meal, and gave Joe his dime.

Colly greeted Ben from the boardwalk outside the Elkhorn as he emerged from the cafe. Her skin shone golden in the sun.

'I'm going to see if Frank's made peace with the sheriff.'

Ben regarded her shrewdly. 'You really have changed sides over Frank, haven't you?'

'Maybe I owe your brother something for misjudging him.'

'Well, you can tell Quayle I'm going seeking one of his missing wagons at Granite Creek. Young Joe tells me it could be carrying dynamite. So try to charm Quayle into action.'

'You don't reckon he works to some make-believe boundary?'

'I've no idea how Quayle works.' Ben crinkled his eyes to peer up the street. 'I only hope he's got a conscience.'

'But we reckoned McCabe's men took half a box of dynamite with them when they abandoned their first wagon.'

'Sure. It'd only need a stick or two to stop a stage at Sunstroke Rocks. Add the rest, and they've more than plenty.'

Colly leant thoughtfully on the boardwalk post. 'Do I detect a glimmer of doubt?'

'Wa-all, something nags me. We never did decide why they brought that first wagon right through Sunstroke.'

'And Granite Creek's hardly on a direct route back.'

'Puzzling. But it might be where I'll find Clipper.'

Clipper found both team horses pegged near a copse of willow beside the wagon. With a struggle he hitched them up. The bright red paint on the wheels was tacky as he touched it.

He glanced across at Nat who lay a few yards away. 'Word from McCabe,' Clipper had greeted the wagon-watcher – then clubbed him with a rock. The effort had left Clipper's heart thudding like hoofbeats; but Nat was out cold.

If only he hadn't lost his matches ... It would have been simple to blow the dynamite sky-high. But Granite Creek was still an ideal spot for losing a wagon into the river. The fast-flowing water came burbling over submerged rocks into the gorge fifty feet below. A congested, rugged place.

Breath sawing, he rested to collect his wits. His whiskery jaw tensed as he cursed McCabe and his men. Scowling, mustering his draining strength, he set about backing the horses to brake the wagon above the overhang. Then he would slap the critters free.

A yard from the brink he paused, wheezing, feeling his lack of experience in manhandling wagons near a cliff edge. Stooping, he glanced underneath and saw a rock jammed against one of the wheels. He straightened up cautiously and hoped he wasn't starting another dizzy spell after that goddam ride.

He applied the brake and unhitched the team. As the horses began to walk forward, he changed his mind. He should be trying further along where there were less stones.

With his trail-grimed bandana, Clipper mopped his face. He had a desolate feeling that he wasn't thinking straight; that destroying the wagon might not be the answer.

Matches! ... Maybe Nat had some. With blurring vision he peered towards the sprawled wagon-watcher. Why the hell hadn't he checked before? Cut out all this sashaying.

'Clipper!' The voice sprang from the willows. 'What the hell you doing with that wagon?'

Clipper swung round. The muzziness in his skull was turning into a sharp pain. He tried to discern the two riders who sat their mounts by the trees. Chub and Lance were they?

As the team continued to step ahead, Clipper

heard the brake slip. The wagon began to roll back from the brink. Its front wheel punched him in the kidney, toppling him. As he scrabbled to sit up he saw Lance grabbing the team.

He did not realise Chub had drawn a gun until the roar of the Colt drowned the drumming in his ears. Clipper lurched backwards. As he hit the ground he recalled McCabe's parting words after ripping the bandage from his brow: 'You'll live ...'

The redness pumping from his chest matched the paint on the wagon and told Clipper he was dying.

# THIRTEEN

After the corduroy road had dwindled into a grassy trail, Ben drew rein to study the foothills. There was only one feature resembling a knoll. He ascended it, then surveyed the barren scene below and across to the opposite ridge. The air carried the cold fragrance and tiny whispers of early spring.

He rode for flatter ground which became criss-crossed with old trails from abandoned claims. He topped a shallow rise, but even the good half of his glasses revealed no sign of human life – only Sparville, some two miles to the south-west.

Presently he heard a faint crack. A shot? He could not be sure. He rowelled the roan, then paused again listening acutely. Was that a wagon rumbling beyond the ridge? The sound faded.

He began to detect a murmuring of water. That must be Granite Creek ahead. Yet he remained puzzled. If the dynamite was destined for Sunstroke Rocks, why bring it out here?

Then as the burbling swelled he caught a glimpse of grey clothing amid the grass. He hastened forward. A man lay unconscious with a large bruise on his head. It was Nat, the lookout who had first challenged him. Nearby a cliff edge overlooked the turbulent water. Then he spotted Clipper.

The sheepherder lay with an arm outflung,

coonskin hat askew. A puddle of congealing blood soaked his vest front.

Ben swung down. From the confused wheel tracks near the cliff edge he guessed that Clipper had been trying to topple the wagon, but there was no sign of it in the creek below.

At first he thought the sheepman was dead. Rolled-up eyeballs glinted white through slit lids. Then he caught a flicker of pupil as though Clipper was trying to focus.

'Clipper?' Ben said quietly. 'Clipper?'

There came a gurgling cough. Ben eased a hand under the sheepman's head, thrusting the coonskin there as a crude pillow.

'Which of 'em did it?' Somehow it hardly mattered. He tried again: 'Clipper, when are they aimin' to use the dynamite?'

A croak broke forth. 'Tonight. After dark.'

*Tonight?* ... Surely that couldn't be right.

'Have they taken the wagon to Sunstroke Rocks?'

The sheepman looked bewildered. Feebly he shook his head.

Ben leant closer. 'But ain't the hold-up to be there?'

Again the weak shake. 'They'll use – hill.'

'Hill? What hill?'

'Back of bank – Sparville.' With a final croak Clipper's head flopped lifelessly over.

As Ben straightened up those last words of the dead sheepman hit home. He cursed himself for not guessing the truth. Blowing a reinforced building explained the need for extra dynamite. *The strongroom's the toughest to reach the west, with the latest in time locks*, Quayle had bragged. Maybe. But McCabe was damn sure gonna try to crack it. Sunstroke Rocks was all moonshine.

The bank should yield a bigger haul. It

explained why McCabe was assembling such a large band. And if he struck after dark, the bank staff should be absent.

Ben recalled the figures scribbled on the bank slip. Could they be a combination to the strongroom? If Renny had hawked them around for two years, they may no longer apply. So McCabe had contacted Bryceman at the bank for up-to-date figures.

Ben covered Clipper's face with the coonskin cap. He felt little remorse. Disapproval of sheepmen was in his bones, yet here was one who had spurned the dubious company he kept. Clipper and Renny. Sheepman, bankman. Both different; both dead.

As Ben pointed the roan back to Sparville, his mind was treading circles. What, he asked himself, did he know about robbing a bank? Too damned little. He would need to scout the layout of the building; need the help that Quayle seemed so reluctant to offer. One thing was sure; he mustn't waste time.

He recalled Charlie Priest's words. *Banks are too sturdy, unless you can bribe someone to leave the strongroom ajar.*

Maybe *that* was Bryceman's role. Then McCabe wouldn't even need a combination. He'd blast the outer wall, then the strongroom would be cleaned out double quick. Yet in his fervour of enthusiasm, Ben had sudden doubt. Would anyone have the gall to rob a bank that way? Surely raiders usually struck in business hours. A few guns herded off the dumbstruck customers; panicky cashiers stuffed their sacks with bills. Then away.

It was almost dark. He wondered who might be driving the dynamite wagon. Probably Chub and one called Lance, going by Joe's information. But would others have joined them yet?

Ben still hadn't seen a likely wagon as he reached the houses and began to cut through poorly lit streets. He could hear distant revellers, but here all seemed quiet.

Clipper had mentioned a hill. Holding the roan to a cautious pace, Ben entered a turning which sloped down to Russet Street behind the bank. A sign told him this was called Hill Street.

Emerging into Russet Street Ben glanced both ways. Still no wagon. All seemed unchanged, even to the roof-repairer's ladder propped against a balcony. His nerves were on edge.

He cantered for Main Street and tied up outside the Elkhorn. Frank had registered but was not in his room. He heard Colly call from the lounge.

'Ben, what kept you?' She looked sleek and lively, still in her rangeriding garb.

'Granite Creek. D'you know where Frank is?'

'He could have gone back to Quayle's office.'

'What, again? He took some pushing last time.'

'There's good reason. Ben, we've found a wagon.'

'You've done what?' He pushed his hat back and stared.

'Me and Frank, an hour ago. We think it's from Wright's sawmill; Quayle mentioned details. And in the store earlier I'd heard some folk discussing it. One oldster who'd been astir around dawn said he thought he'd seen it moving into Russet Street. When I told Frank we decided to poke around at dusk, looking for it. He could be informing Quayle about it right now; he's anxious to keep on the sheriff's best side ... Did you find your dynamite wagon, Ben? No? Then come, I'll show you ours.'

Confidently, Colly led him into the dingy streets. For the moment he said nothing. The sawmill wagon seemed a digression until they reached a padlocked gate set in a high fence.

'Look through one of those cracks,' she murmured. 'Well?'

'There's a wagon and team in there, sure.' Ben frowned. 'And we're in Russet Street not far from the rear of the bank.'

'We'd passed this gate when two men came along. One was gingery, spoke like a French-Canadian. Frank said he'd seen him with McCabe's bunch by the corral. So we kept watch.'

'You mean they went through the gate? Had they a key?'

'Yes. They locked up on leaving.' Colly's eyes gleamed. 'We guessed they'd been leaving the horses some oats.'

'Yeah, the critters are chomping now in their nosebags.' Ben fingered the padlock. 'This looks brand new. Whose yard is it anyway?'

'It's private. It backs on to the billiard hall.'

'Did either of you check what's on the wagon?'

'No.' Colly's voice rose. 'Ben, steady – where – ?'

He was springing for the top of the fence. He swung himself over. 'Whistle if anyone comes, then vamoose.'

He dropped nimbly down. One of the horses nickered in its feed-bag. He calmed it with soothing words, then quickly inspected the wagon, lifting back a draped tarpaulin. Satisfied, he made a swift exit, Colly stood waiting anxiously.

'It's the Wright's wagon, no doubt. The name's on the side. And there's a load under the tarp. I don't mean dynamite. Empty carpetbags. Didn't Quayle mention some were stolen today? There's even a few gunny sacks among 'em. We'd best move from here.'

Colly walked in appraising silence. 'So where in tarnation's your dynamite? Gone to Sunstroke Rocks?'

'No. McCabe intends using it to rob the bank.'

Ben added details about finding Clipper. 'And the raid's tonight.'

'Oh, no,' she said in dismay. 'Quayle was going to put Grandpa's gold in a deposit box for me this afternoon.'

'One box among many. McCabe must intend those carpetbags for shifting the haul. The dynamite wagon ain't arrived yet. I reckon it drew aside somewhere, biding time.'

As they reached Main Street, Ben faltered, his features tense in the glow of a hanging kerosene lamp.

'Colly, you'd better go back to the Elkhorn.'

'Why? Ben, I don't want you doing anything rash.'

'Do I ever?' He forced a tight grin. 'Stay out of this, Colly. It ain't your game.'

'With Grandpa's gold in the bank?' Spots of umbrage glowed on her cheeks. 'It's as much my game as yours, Ben Galliard.'

Ben relented. 'Then can you see to my hoss? I'm going to stir Quayle off his butt. If you see Frank before I do, tell him what's happened. He offered help, and I'm gonna need it.'

As Ben stalked along he shook his head vigorously, trying to clear his thoughts. He still had no proof of Bryceman's role. Nor did he know the proposed time of the raid.

Quayle's office was locked. Ben thumped on the adjoining door. He was losing track of time, but already the town was quiet. He felt himself an outcast, about to face trial in a burg which he did not even represent. A maverick marshal.

A surly growl broke from the back premises. 'Who is it?'

'Ben Galliard. Can I come in and talk? It's important.'

There came a subdued cursing. Presently a bolt was withdrawn. Quayle peered out ghoulishly over a lamp. He looked like he had just pulled his pants on. 'What the hell time d'you call this?'

'Late.' Without ceremony Ben thrust his way in.

'This had better be worth hearing.' Reluctantly Quayle led him along the passage and dumped the lamp down on to a table.

Ben faced him. 'That robbery won't be at Sunstroke Rocks. It's at the bank. And not next week; it's tonight.'

Quayle stared. 'Are you plumb crazy? I told you that strongroom's foolproof, with an up-to-date time lock.'

'But if Bryceman leaves it open or' – a fresh thought struck Ben – 'sets it to unlock itself during the night –'

'Bryceman? What's he got to do with it –'

'If McCabe got Bryceman's name from Renny he could have cooked up a deal. So – where does Bryceman live?'

Quayle hesitated. 'Suppose you tell me first about Granite Creek. The Wells woman said you'd gone scouting there.'

'For Truscott's wagon.' Ben gave a quick account of finding the dying Clipper. 'The wagon's on its way back somewhere, ready to blow the bank open. Now, can you roust up some reliable guns?'

'I can't rush up a cordon in two minutes –'

'Goddammit, can't you grasp what I'm saying?' Ben smacked the table top, making the lamp flicker.

Quayle looked mildly astonished. 'Where they gonna stash this dynamite anyway?'

'Hill Street is my guess. If they let the wagon run downhill some eighty yards with fuses burning it'll hit the back of the bank. When that blows, they'll move in mob-handed.'

'But ...' The sheriff rubbed his face, floundering.
Ben added: 'That sawmill wagon ain't so far away either.'
'Yeah, Russet Street. Your brother told me –'
'But Frank didn't check what's on it. Your missing carpetbags; and sacks. All handy for scooping up the strongroom loot. Now – where the hell do I find Bryceman. He should know the deadline.'
'Grade Street, near the bank. Number seventeen. But –'
'Then you roust your men up, pronto. I wanna see things moving by the time I get back.'

Ben banged on Bryceman's door. He heard a startled male voice – 'Who the hell's that?' – and the squeal of a woman.
'Marshal Galliard.' Ben made no pretence at good manners. 'Open up.' He undid the tie-down on his holster.
'Who? Never heard of you.'
An argument began. 'See what he wants,' the woman said.
After some bumbling about a florid man in shirt and pants cracked the door open. 'What the – ?' He staggered aside as Ben pushed in. In a room on the left a frowsy blonde jerked the antimacassar off a sofa to cover her breasts. Ben ignored her.
'Bryceman? I hear we got a bank raid lined up.'
'What? Hey, who said you could come bustin' in –?'
'I want to know what time we can expect things to happen.' Ben thrust the muzzle of his .45 close to Bryceman's head, causing the woman to yelp in alarm. 'And I want to know now.'
'What are you talking about?' Bryceman turned a sickly grey. Behind the sofa a second woman crouched in her camisole.
The blonde began to screech. 'Don't shoot him.'

To Bryceman she babbled: 'Tell him or he'll kill you. Tell him.'

Ben waited. Bryceman sagged quivering against a chair. 'I'm no bank raider. I'm employed there –'

'Damn right. So was Renny. Did McCabe tell you he's dead?' As the women backed towards the sideboard, Ben slid the muzzle over Bryceman's cheekbone. 'Look, I ain't particular which of these dolls I splatter your brains over ... How's the strongroom positioned?'

Bryceman licked dry lips with a tacky tongue. 'In the centre down some steps –'

'So it'll protect the contents when McCabe blasts his way in from Russet Street? What about the combination number?'

'I – he don't need that. I set the timer to unlock.'

Ben nodded. As he'd figured. 'Unlock when?'

'About three in the morning.'

So, Ben thought – there was not long to go.

'And you think no one'll suspect you when they find the strongroom lock undamaged?'

Bryceman supported himself on the table. 'Easy with that gun. How can I talk if you keep jabbing me?' He sucked in a trembling breath. 'When McCabe clears the contents he's gonna blow a charge against the lock to divert suspicion –'

Ben smiled pityingly. 'Bryceman, you're a bigger idiot than you look. McCabe's concern will be getting the hell out. Not diverting suspicion. If you want to save your skin, we go to the bank now and make that strongroom door secure again.'

'I can't do that. The manager keeps the front door keys. And he was going late-night visiting.'

'Then the sooner we start seeking him, the better.'

Nudging with the Colt, ignoring the women who were clinging together, Ben shoved Bryceman out of the house.

Before they had covered a dozen yards three shadows darted from an alley. Ben jerked aside instinctively, colliding with a downpipe from some overheard guttering. Before he could twist his gun-hand round something clanged at the crown of his head. As he slumped amid a spangle of lights he glimpsed Bryceman being slugged to the ground. Then he was slithering into oblivion.

# FOURTEEN

When Ben found his feet his head was thumping with anger at his own stupidity. It was only sense that McCabe would have Bryceman watched until after the raid. Whoever had seen them leaving the house together had decided to take no chances.

Lurching straddle-legged, Ben cursed the sonsofbitches. He felt like his skull had been kicked by a mule.

Tripping over a wooden baton he grabbed for the rim of a rainwater butt beneath the downcome. As he fought the waves of nausea, he found splinters clinging to his jacket. The baton, luckily, had been rotten, its blow cushioned by the pipe.

His right hand was numb. From the way his knuckles were swelling, he guessed someone had trodden on it. He picked his hat up, scooped some rainwater from the butt, and sloshed it over his head. As the wet shock revived him he saw his Colt lying behind the butt. He was lifting it gingerly when he noticed Bryceman sprawled inside the alley. He moved across to check.

The bank ... That was his major concern.

He was just emerging from the alley when he heard footsteps and female voices. Colly was approaching. And with her – Bryceman's two wanton women.

'Colly, what brings you along?'

'Ben! These – ladies found you lying and were

seeking help.'

'We were looking for Mr Bryceman,' the blonde corrected her. 'This marshal hauled him out, then we heard a shindy outside —'

'Your fancy man's in the alley,' Ben said.

The women turned. 'Sweet Jesus!' They scurried to help him.

Colly was reaching for Ben's bruised hand. 'McCabe's men? What have they done? How can you use a gun — ?'

'Now don't start hollerin' "Doctor". I don't want hamstringing with bandages. Besides, they didn't do a very thorough job.' Ben glanced about. 'What time is it?'

'Must be all of two o'clock.'

'Time to move.' Leaving the women to care for Bryceman, Ben hurried Colly away. 'How did you meet up with those two?'

'I got restless. Frank hadn't appeared, so I was going looking. Then these flustered women came out of Grade Street.'

'They'd been with Bryceman, McCabe's bank contact. The raid's due around three. Colly, help me to adjust this gunbelt.'

Ben positioned the belt to bring the holster forward for a left-hand crossdraw. Colly regarded it dubiously.

'I'm ambidextrous,' he reassured her. 'Can you check for Frank back at the Elkhorn? Ask him to meet me at Quayle's.'

There was a lamp glowing in the sheriff's office. As Ben stalked in, Quayle glanced up from checking some hand weapons.

'You took your time.' There was a querulous note in Quayle's voice. 'Did you learn anything from Bryceman?'

'Bryceman's out cold.' Ben explained what had happened. 'But he said the strongroom should unlock itself at three. So the dynamite should be arriving just after.' He looked at the wall clock. 'That gives us twenty minutes. Laycock should know how to reset the time lock, but first you got to find him.'

'I ain't placing men inside the bank, if that's your notion.' Quayle rubbed his chin morosely. 'And these Colts could do with greasing before I issue any.'

Ben gritted his teeth in frustration. 'Quayle, ain't you got no further than greasing guns?'

'I got a deputy seeking extras. We're meeting in ten minutes ... Did Bryceman say nothing else?'

'Nothing. He was taking a dip in the cracker-barrel with a coupla soiled doves. Look, time's running short.'

'Yeah.' Overcoming his inertia, Quayle began to strap on his gunbelt. 'Any sighting yet of that dynamite wagon?'

'How the hell do I know? I ain't had chance to look.' As Ben turned for the door, Quayle snatched up a bunch of keys.

'Hold on. Don't go rushing out. If it's helpers you want ...' Quayle pushed through a dividing door to the jailhouse.

Ben followed, then halted as the sheriff began to unlock one of the cells. 'What in hell's name —?'

'Howdy, Ben.' Frank pushed his hat off his face and swung his feet off a truckle bed. 'You sure pick some meeting places.'

Ben glared at Quayle. 'You're doing some damned funny things. What's the idea juggin' Frank again?'

'He ain't locked up for shooting Eli Dunn. This was his idea. Precaution. Some cronies of Eli still ain't satisfied, so we decided he'd be safer in here tonight.'

'Plus the sheriff's still sore about me filching his

keys.' Frank yawned and shrugged. 'Plus I brought tidings of his sawmill wagon. Has Colly told you? With McCabe's men giving oats to the team, I thought I was doing our sheriff a favour.'

Quayle appealed to Ben: 'For all I knew he could have been telling me about the Wright's wagon to convince me he's not in cahoots with McCabe. But as soon as I question it he gets uppity and volunteers himself back into the cell.'

'Yeah,' Frank drawled. 'I've decided to recline in luxury.'

'You picked a damned fine night to do it,' Ben grated. 'McCabe's raiding the bank in ten minutes.'

Frank tilted an eyebrow in mild surprise. 'That a fact?'

'Damn right. The best way to show you ain't linked with McCabe is to help us tackle him.'

'Plausible.' Frank began to pull his boots on. 'So do I get my gun back now, Quayle, you crafty old sidewinder? Colt Frontier, cedarwood butt. You been holding it for two weeks.'

'Ah.' Quayle's memory jolted. 'You want to get your sweet self gunned down, that's your affair.' To Ben, he said: 'I was only keeping him on ice still I'd examined the Wright's wagon.' Holding the cell door open, he jerked a thumb. 'Make the weasel sweat. He's all yours.'

At the sheriff's lack of grace. Ben's right fist was bunching. He had a firm feeling that Quayle was subtly outsmarting him. Then his swollen knuckles imparted a jab of caution. Punching Quayle on the jaw would hardly help.

In his office, Quayle unlocked a cupboard. He lugged out a shellbelt with a holstered Colt Frontier .45, jerked a pad forward and pointed to his ink bottle. 'Sign.'

As Frank got the scratchy pen to work, Ben exploded at Quayle: 'Damned procedures! How about some action?'

'I don't see what you're complaining about,' Quayle barked.

'Look, Quayle, I no more want to tackle McCabe than you do. I never wanted to be Bleak Springs marshal. I sure as hell don't wanna be a Sparville sheriff.' Ben choked back his wrath. 'You'll find us near the bank when you've collected your men.'

Ben hurried alongside his brother, too incensed to speak. Frank threw him a glance. 'I thought these bastards were gonna rob a stage.'

'That was Cricklewood's plan. McCabe's is to run a dynamite wagon into the back of the bank. Blow the wall.'

'They're shifting a whole bank load?' Frank said, as they cut through minor streets. 'How long's that gonna take them?'

'Not long if the strongroom's open. That sawmill wagon's loaded with carpetbags and sacks for a quick clean-out.'

Frank peered around, muttering. 'Which street are we in?'

'This brings us to the top of Hill Street.' A moment later, Ben touched Frank's arm. 'There!' He gestured ahead.

Three men were uncoupling a wagon team. One man climbed up by the seat, and Ben could hear the scuffling and clopping as the other two coaxed the horses away to a safer spot.

'You cut across the road,' Ben whispered. 'Circuit round to the far side.' Frank moved off as stealthy as a catamount.

Ben drew nearer. The man on the wagon kept one restraining hand on the brake handle. A lamp on the seat cast a feeble glow on the scene. The explosive seemed to be covered by tarps and there were blurred clumps that could have been straw.

Ben heard liquid being dribbled and detected the odour of kerosene. The man gestured 'all set' to his helpmates and prepared to jump. A match flared.

'Hold it!' Ben darted forward. The man jerked round, but not before touching the match to a fuse.

That same instant, shadows shifted in a doorway. Cursing, Ben threw himself aside as a gunshot crashed. Then all hell was raging.

Ben pumped his first shot at the villain on the wagon, sprawling him into the road amid a scattering of dynamite sticks. Frank picked off the man in the doorway. The other two men dove for cover, their presence registering as flame stabs of gunfire. As the brake slithered free the wagon began to roll downslope.

Ben sensed a lull, as though all were watching the receding glow. Fusecord and lamp provided double assurance in case either one failed.

The wagon crunched to a halt amid splintering boards. The lamp pitched off the seat into the fuel-soaked straw. A thunderous flash of orange came on cue as wagon and bank wall errupted into boiling flame, rending timber and flying masonry.

'Glory to hell,' Ben breathed in dismay. From cover of darkness he heard Frank's voice, low across the street:

'Ain't that what we were supposed to prevent?'

Before the rubble had ceased to fall more shadows emerged, hastening downhill. Some fired randomly towards Ben and Frank. But right then the lure of booty was taking preference.

Where was Quayle? Darkness was dispelled by blazing straw. Lights were brightening in windows; half the town was rousing.

Ben held his fire. He needed to be sure of his targets. Of the other two rogues from the wagon, one lay prone; the other was staggering sideways painfully clutching his belly.

The explosion had done more than rupture the wall. The complete rear face of the bank had collapsed. Ben could see part of a ceiling hanging. Raiders were already scrambling in, scarcely hampered by the rubble and burning fragments. As he'd guessed, some carried carpetbags and sacks.

Frank appeared from the gloom, snatching up a fallen stick of dynamite. 'Souvenir,' he said.

They dodged down Hill Street, hugging opposite walls. The nearer the bank, the harder it became to remain unseen.

A clatter of wheels came from Russet Street. A cussing wagonman was trying to steer his panicky horses closer to the shattered wall. Men were scurrying from the bank with loaded containers. The time lock must have operated on schedule.

Ben sprinted closer. He heard Quayle's voice coming from along Russet Street: 'You men drop your guns –'

Derisive shouts, an exchange of shots. Quayle's helpers must be limited in number. Ben restricted his targets to those firelit figures in the demolished wall space. Four villains were hand-chaining sacks out over the rubble from those inside the strongroom. An outward-facing rank was keeping Quayle's men pinned down. Ben dove into a doorway, returning fire as lead spattered around him, then fumbled to reload.

The getaway wagon was now brimming with loot: sacks, deposit boxes, carpetbags crammed with valuables. Within moments it would be away. Gunmen were riding their nags from the streets. Smart planning, Ben judged grimly. He'd credit McCabe with that.

He dropped another man and saw one fall to a fusillade from Quayle; but anguished yells from along Russet Street told him that Quayle's guns were also taking punishment.

'Frank, where the hell are you?' Ben called, anxious about his brother's silence.

Then Frank was hurrying forward. 'Keep me covered.'

As Ben slammed more rounds at the crouching gunnies, Frank lobbed his souvenir dynamite stick – then staggered, clutching his leg. Fuse sizzling, the dynamite soared towards the sagging roof. It exploded, giving the overhang the nudge it needed.

Ben heard screams as men were buried in a havoc of showering rafters and bricks. He seized the moment to climb on to a keg, then via a ledge to a more commanding position on a corner balcony. The wagon horses were squealing and shying as the teamster fought to control them.

And Ben caught the unmistakable voice of McCabe.

'Leave the rest. Let's get to hell out.'

# FIFTEEN

Escape was now priority for McCabe. Any loot not loaded up became ignored. Frank's hurling of the dynamite had still failed to thwart several raiders. Ben could see the wagon pulling out towards the debris scattered in the road.

'Nice try, Frank,' Ben muttered, more to himself. 'Kinda late.' He glanced about. Where was his brother lurking now?

Several of the gunnies' nags were shying as final shots were exchanged. Ben crouched for cover behind his balcony rail, overlooking both Hill and Russet Street. The raiders seemed to have lost sight of him.

Any moment now, the wagon would rattle away. He took careful aim at the teamster. A click told him that his Colt was empty.

Ben cursed. He must halt the wagon. He owed that to Frank. Where was the man? ... The wagon was hugging the building beneath, forced there by the rubble. Ben looked about. Was there nothing he could hurl to delay it?

Two balconies along he saw the roof-repairer's ladder.

The whip thrashing the horses had his eyes on the road. Ben took the six-foot gap to the next balcony in an acrobatic leap, managing to grab hold and hang on. The wagon was almost past him. He felt a selfish moment of thanks that Quayle's group was drawing the gunfire. Running along, he leapt for the second balcony and kicked at the ladder, then realised it was rope-lashed to the rail. He whipped out his Bowie and with one swift slice parted the strands. He footed the ladder free.

Its top struck a window opposite, smashing glass and bringing the centre rungs just above horsehead level. They slammed into the startled wagonman's chest. As the ladder top wedged into the window jamb the wagon slewed to a standstill. Four mounted raiders behind it halted in confusion.

Ben seized the moment to reload. Spying him, the wheeling riders below launched an upward hail of lead. As Ben sniped back, more guns were trading shots across Hill Street.

Ben clung to the balcony floor. In the dim glow he glimpsed the sheen of a claybank underneath. The critter pranced with a fierce grace, too noble for the rider astride it.

'Grab a bag,' McCabe snapped, and reached into the wagon. Snatching the biggest sack to hand, he jumped the claybank over the foot of the ladder, hugging the wall to thwart Ben's aim. Three more riders took the jump, among them Chub. Ben winged one of the others in the shoulder. A fourth was following when a down-street bullet threw him from the saddle. McCabe and his three accomplices galloped away, each clutching a sack.

The gunfire sputtered out. 'Get across leather,' Quayle ordered his men. 'Get after 'em!' He called up: 'Galliard, is that you on that balcony? You want to ride with 'em?'

Ben declined. 'I'll need to sort out my hoss.'

'What about your brother?'

'What about me?' Frank came limping from Hill street, leaning on the wall. 'I'd have been safer staying in jail.'

'Less of your sass,' the sheriff retorted.

As a helper offered Frank a supporting shoulder, Ben pushed through the balcony door and down into the street.

Outside a thin crowd was gathering. A horse-drawn appliance trundled up. Two men began to operate a hand pump.

'Tardy wisdom.' Ben watched them damping down the last of the burning straw. But he was glad of their presence.

He turned to Frank. 'How many wounds are you licking?'

'Just one in the leg.' Frank stifled a wince.

'You'd better have it looked at.'

Quayle was taking tally – present, missing and casualties. 'One man dead, three wounded – two seriously.' He nodded grimly. 'Against that several of McCabe's scum are dead.'

'Arrests?' Ben asked.

'Eight so far. Gave 'emselves up in the end.'

Quayle turned to the stalled wagon where two of his men were extricating the unconscious teamster from the ladder. He peered at the load. 'Any sign of Mr Laycock yet?'

A stressed bank manager push forward. 'This is awful.' He shook his muttonchop whiskers. 'The strongroom's empty.'

'Relax,' said Quayle. 'Most of the contents are still here. McCabe was too greedy. If they'd settled for just a sack each –'

'Four of 'em did,' said Ben. 'McCabe and three others.' He turned to Laycock. 'Looks like you'll have to shore the place up more'n somewhat,' he said in understatement.

Quayle glared at Ben. His eyes were cold and malignant. 'Tinhorn marshal. You were supposed to prevent all this.'

'Listen, Quayle.' Ben felt his hackles rising. 'If

you'd moved your ass we might have nipped the full shebang in the bud instead of just being late on the scene.'

As he swung away in disgust, two riders came drumming in from the east, the front man swaying. 'Kirk's hurt,' someone called. Ben could see blood on the lolling man's coat.

'What's happened?' Quayle demanded.

Breathless, the second rider reined his snorting horse. 'The sonsofbitches jumped us. Bart and Joel are dead.'

'Jesus Christ!' Quayle began to rage. 'There were five of you. Where's Martin? Didn't you get any of 'em?'

Contritely the rider shook his head. 'They shot Martin's hoss from under him. He's lying with a hip wound –'

'You rubberbrains!' Quayle detailed a party to collect the dead and wounded. 'And bring 'em in; don't join 'em.'

While the sheriff issued more orders for guarding the strongroom, Ben sat on a step testing the edge on his Bowie. Presently Quayle simmered down and stuck his thumbs in his belt.

'Anyway,' he concluded, 'we didn't do too bad. Scum like that – they're always taking too much on.'

Ben held a crooked smile, but said nothing. Let Quayle do the crowing, reap the glory. It was his town. To hell with what others might have done.

Ben nursed only one regret – McCabe, Chub and two others had hightailed out with four sacks of loot.

A half hour later Ben stood with one foot propped on a collapsed beam, talking to the distraught bank chief.

'So you'll keep the strongroom and rebuild round it?'

'We think so,' Laycock said. 'Make it foolproof

again.'

Ben was tempted to ask if it was foolproof before. He drew aside to find Colly pushing through the crowd.

'Ben, are you hurt? I wish I could have helped –'

'Smouldering here and there.' His mouth tasted like charred timber, but he managed a grin.

Colly surveyed the wreckage. 'What a hopeless mess.'

'Yeah. We don't deserve any medals, but most of the money's secure – apart from four bags McCabe took.'

Laycock was lavishing praise on the sheriff: 'Commendable effort. Yes, sir! Even better, now I know about Bryceman. We'll see that Sparville can still keep its trust in the bank.'

'Who's he trying to convince?' Ben muttered to Colly.

'I just spoke with your brother,' she said. 'The doctor was taking a slug from his leg, back of the mercantile store.'

'So he may not be riding for a day or two.' Ben turned to Quayle. 'What you gonna do about the four who escaped?'

'Do?' Quayle made a braggart gesture. 'I'm gonna do plenty. I'll circulate news on McCabe far and wide –'

'What about the townfolk he's killed?'

The sheriff looked solemn. 'Dead men are dead ... But you can tell that brother of yours I still got a bone to pick.'

'Frank's carrying a leg wound.' Ben fed him a blank stare and worked his bruised hand. 'And now it's my turn for the doc.'

With a neat new plaster adorning his hand, Ben tracked Frank down in a rooming house near the wrecked bank. Frank was resting his leg and chewing on a match.

'So you ain't hobbling back to the Elkhorn? I'm hoping to head back to Bleak Springs tomorrow after breakfast.'

'That so? I'd have ridden with you,' Frank apologized, 'but the doc says I ought to rest for a coupla days.'

'Sure,' Ben agreed, 'but don't take any truck from Quayle.'

'If he tries sticking me back in the lock-up I'll sit him ass-first on his spurs. Is the Wells girl riding with you?'

'Early to say. I don't want to loiter here too long.'

Frank grimaced, easing his sore shin. 'You ain't figgering on settling in Bleak as marshal?'

'Nope. I told you, I'm here to lure you home. But McCabe'll be wanting me good and dead. He'll guess I'll be reporting back to Bleak, so that could be where he'll try for it.'

'Well, stay safe, Ben,' said Frank, with rare concern. 'Why not wait a couple more days till I can join you?'

'No. You'll have to follow on when you're mended.'

Ben called back at the sheriff's office where a deputy helped him to check the jailed gunmen for faces and names. 'There could still be one or two missing,' the deputy said.

Somewhat uneasy, Ben returned to the ruined bank where Laycock and Quayle were discussing security measures. Colly had returned to the hotel. Quayle picked his way across.

'Galliard? Did you tell your brother I wanted to see him?'

'Why? Did you want to recommend him for a decoration?'

'Now don't try that frisky talk with me.' Quayle's eyes gleamed in defiance. 'He was supposed to be helping, not tossing dynamite. Both Mr Laycock and myself saw him hurl that stick. And I still ain't satisfied he'd no personal interest.'

Ben was briefly speechless. 'What in tarnation are you raving about? He stopped one in the leg, didn't he?'

Quayle's mouth locked in a smirk, as though he was duped by his own argument. 'Forget it then.' He turned away.

'No, we won't forget it.' Ben snatched at his shoulder. 'Frank threw that stick to drop the ceiling on those jaspers.'

'That's your version. Maybe he mistimed it –'

Quayle's words ended in a strangled grunt as Ben yanked him one-handed up on to his toes.

'Some day you'll need to mend your suspicions.' Ben spoke through clenched teeth. 'You've boxed me from the word go. You bounce Frank in and out of choky. You only moved your ass to stop the townfolk ripping your precious carpet out from under your feet. And now you're hinting Frank's in cahoots with McCabe. Quayle, you stink like a ruptured skunk.'

Ben sprawled the dumbstruck sheriff back into the debris. Checked by his throbbing hand, he stalked away to the hotel.

Healthier for sleep, Ben left his room for a late breakfast with Colly. 'We won't waste time starting out,' he told her. 'Frank's hoping to follow us later.'

After collecting their mounts and picking up provisions they rode out past the wagoner's. Joe was leaning on his broom. He gave a rueful smile. 'Riding back to Bleak now, marshal?'

'Reckon so. You're looking busy, Joe. Heard anything new?'

'One of the men who got bushwhacked when those raiders escaped – he said he heard the one on the claybank claiming he'd drop you dead first chance.' Joe regarded Ben with concerned eyes. 'You ain't gonna let him do that, are you?'

'No fear. Though he'd sure like to try.'

Colly smiled her reassurance. 'None of 'em stand a chance, Joe. Not while Ben keeps a full chamber on his hogleg.'

Ben wished he felt so sure of himself.

'Thanks for your help, Joe.' He lifted the reins. 'But don't let Mr Fergus see you squashing those bristles. 'Cause if I ever come back we might need that broom to sweep Sparville clean of gun-totin' varmints.'

Joe grinned. They left him sweeping with renewed vigour.

# SIXTEEN

As Ben and Colly rode out at a steady clip, Ben examined his feelings. His achievements in Sparville had been far from perfect. Law-abiding men had been killed.

'Colly, you're taking this kinda lightly,' he ventured.

'And you're too much on edge.' She threw him a smile.

Ben recognised too well his own unease. From now McCabe might avoid robbery in the bigger towns, but not the smaller ones like Bleak Springs. And Ben was top of McCabe's hit-list.

They took the upper trail. Ben clenched at the reins. All this speculation was leaving him soured inside.

There was Chub, the artful roper. But who were the other two with McCabe? Curly perhaps. Or the second lookout from the hollow – who Ben figgered could be the one called Lance. Ben wished he could be certain there were no others on the loose.

They made camp at dusk. Ben remained broody. While Colly prepared supper, he sat to one side testing the speed of his draw. He caught Colly watching him, and he put his gun away.

Next day, when they resumed the trail, Colly said: 'I guess young Joe was right to be concerned for you.'

'I thought you talked him out of that.'

'Maybe I did. Or maybe I talked myself into it.'

Nearer Bleak Springs, Ben reined in as a rider approached. 'It's Doctor Mason,' Colly said. They waited. Some two miles away, Bleak's few buildings looked deserted.

The doctor cantered up, muffled in his mackinaw coat. 'Morning to you. Have you completed your business?'

'Sort of.' Ben gave an acid smile. 'But Sunstroke Rocks was a wrong steer.'

'Ben means he fought off a bank raid in Sparville,' Colly explained. 'He's hoping to catch up with McCabe and three others who escaped.'

Mason gazed back towards the buildings. 'Four men rode in this morning. I thought I recognised McCabe. And Curly. A third one was addressed as Lance. Ain't sure of the fourth.'

'Probably Chub.' Ben nodded. 'That's helpful anyway.'

'What happened to those rascals I patched up?'

'Clipper and Renny? Feeding the worms, I guess.'

Mason sighed. 'I could see that coming. There's a chilly atmosphere in town. Folk are staying off the street.'

'I ought to be there. Where are these four men now?'

'They called for a meal, but that was a while back. I'd be cautious. We put Charlie Priest's cross up in the cemetery. We don't want any more. Davison has your office key.'

Mason rode on. Nearer the buildings Ben halted the roan.

'Colly, we ought to split up ... Now don't start playing dumb. I wouldn't want you snarled up in a shootout.'

'I can goddam take care of myself. I did it before

with that mountain cat.' She leant down to slap at her Winchester.

'These are men; not cats. Besides, it ain't your fight.'

'You banning me from town marshal? I reckon I could beat you into Bleak as easy as pitchin' horseshoes.'

Ben faced her. 'Listen, you female firebrand. What's so important that you gotta ride in with me? It won't make 'em any less trigger-happy, you being alongside.'

Colly hesitated. 'No, maybe you're right.'

'So we're agreed? ... Now, wait till I reach yonder rock then start to follow. Not too close. If you spot any sudden movements give me a holler and dive for cover.'

'Understood,' she submitted. 'But I'm keeping my friend ready.' And she patted the Winchester again.

Passing the rock, Ben glanced back. Colly nudged the mare forward. For a moment he wondered if he was being unfair. Then he pushed soul-searching aside to concentrate on staying alive.

He peeled off his gauntlets and blew on his fingers. He undid the tie-down on his holster but kept both hands in view, not wishing to tempt fate. Although he had come out top of one gunfight in Bleak, no one would be hankering for him to start another. And he had the townfolk to consider.

Where was everyone? The place was mantled by an eerie quiet. Had McCabe herded the townfolk aside, or had they sought cover?

Ben still felt he did not belong here. His return seemed marred by personal vendetta. He paused. In the chill, bracing air he could feel a warmth of Montana sun on his back. He wiped his sweat-filmed lip cautiously on his bandana.

With honed senses he took in the fronts of the frame buildings. Drifting aromas began to reach him from saloon and eating house; even an odour of leather from the saddler's. Disuse and decay tainted the street.

First on his right was the deserted signwriter's, then an empty lot or two, all favouring an in-town bushwhack. Or would McCabe position his gunnies nearer to the marshal's office?

Set back to the left was the abandoned *CLARION* shell. Ben rode on. He passed the shuttered clothier's and general store; then more relics including a closed-down cafe.

Three horses were tied nearby. A dappled grey – maybe Chub's? A sorrel, a paint. Could that be Lance's, and the sorrel Curly's? But no sign of a claybank ... Ben scoured from ground to rooftop, sweeping right and left. Gables, false-fronts, nooks and hidey-holes. He saw nothing. The roan pressed slowly on.

He scanned lower storeys. Posts, niches, angles, the crawl-space under the boardwalk. Rain butt, water trough –

'Ben!'

At Colly's shout, Ben swerved in the saddle. He glimpsed a hatbrim protruding overhead. A man clinging to the roof was sighting a sixgun. As Ben whipped out his Colt the man jerked and slid, releasing a shot that missed by inches. And Ben heard the crash of Colly's rifle. He held his weapon cocked but the shoulder visible above the gable had become very still.

Ben glanced all ways. He saw Colly brandishing her rifle like an Indian brave and pulling the mare behind the signwriter's. He flipped a finger in thanks, but doubted if she noticed.

He caught a flash of yellow – the claybank? – towards the printing house. Then his attention was snatched by a scraping noise. Near the saloon a rifle was sliding out beneath the boardwalk steps. He loosed a wild round as he dove from the roan towards the northern sidewalk, rolling under some collapsed boards. Flattening on to his stomach, he brought up his iron exchanging lead with the rifle. From across the street came a throttled gasp. The rifle tilted; the man behind it went prone.

Ben guessed this must be Lance. But where was McCabe? Was he waiting to see how his cohorts scored first?

Ben crawled further in till he was under the crumbling floor of the cafe. He heaved himself up through a gap. From what he recalled there could be an unsecured door out back.

As he paused he detected a scratching from overhead. He crouched by the counter, tensed and listening, trying to pierce the upper gloom for details. Stairway, banister, stacked boxes –

A plummetting crate struck him on the shoulder and crashed onwards through the floor. Scrambling aside, he picked out a glint of metal under the skylight. He jerked up his Colt. Both guns roared together. He felt the sting as his sleeve was ripped; then he was dodging a falling body. It thudded down across a floorboard joist. Silence, then a dripping of blood.

It was Chub. 'Try shooting first next time,' Ben muttered. But there would be no next time for the dead roper.

Ben wiped spiderwebs from his face, checked his Colt, then checked himself. The arm wound was mainly a skin scratch. He made a wary circuit from the rear exit towards the street, then something on the roof grabbed his attention. The buzzard that Colly had picked off was staging a come-back. With a boot heel wedged into the gable he was struggling to lift his gun.

'Don't try it, kid,' Ben called.

As lead spattered down, he released a single shot. The youth cartwheeled off an awning to slam headfirst at the boardwalk. Ben strode over, and recognised Curly. The youth's neck was broken. Ben shook his head in futility. Why couldn't these young bucks choose a saner way of living?

A movement behind brought him spinning round. When he found Colly approaching swinging her rifle, he let his tension rip.

'Goddammit, Colly. D'you have to sneak out like that?'

'Sorry, Ben.' She tried to quell the trembling in her voice. Her body was shaking. 'Are you safe?'

'Safe? I'm standing. I still ain't taken full tally.'

'Don't think bad of me.' Her eyes were splintering with tears. 'After that opening shot, I couldn't carry on –'

'Hell, girl, you weren't meant to.' He laid an arm around her shoulder. 'If it's any comfort, you never killed that varmint. I just finished him off.' Yet his attention was only partly on her. He pushed her towards the nearest building.

'Ben, what is it?' she said in alarm.

'Quiet. We ain't finished yet. I've settled for three, so why ain't the town coming to life? And where's McCabe?'

Ben suddenly felt vulnerable again. He thought back to the head-count he had done in Sparville. Quayle's deputy had reckoned one or two raiders were still unaccounted for. What if they too had reached Bleak Springs by some devious route? That could explain the hush that overlay the town.

Ben crossed cautiously to the south side of the street, then beckoned Colly over. He gestured her into a decrepit doorway while he topped up the shells in his Colt.

An instant later a shot crashed out from the north side. Close to Ben's head, woodwork splintered.

'Holy cows,' Colly breathed. 'That was no pop-gun.'

'The door. Quick.' It swung inwards at Colly's touch. Ben tumbled inside after her as a second shot followed the first. 'Can you see where it's coming from?'

'No. You reckon it's McCabe?'

'Got to be.' Ben pulled a sliver of wood from his jacket fabric. 'This rate, he's gonna owe me a full wardrobe.' He peered through a smeary window. 'I thought I glimpsed his hoss earlier, near the old printing house.'

'If he's back there he's set himself a long-range target.'

'With a rifle that hardly matters, you know damn well. Those first three got their chance and lost. McCabe was probably hoping to pick me off on the office threshold.'

Two more shots came splintering into the building. Ben wished for his Springfield, but it was still in its scabbard on the roan. Besides, he needed a sure sighting. He began to sift his way through rubbish and broken glass. With Colly following, he found the rear exit.

'My guess is there are one or two more jaspers around, herding the townfolk in some place. I'm gonna look around. You stay here, under cover.'

'Ben, be careful.'

He hurried off at a running crouch, sixgun readied. As he passed behind the Blue Norther a soft voice called: 'Marshal.'

Ben span round. He eased a breath of relief on finding the barman peeping through a picket fence and wielding a shotgun.

'Billy, what's been happening?'

'I been watching through the top shutters. That bastard you dropped off the roof was one of those card players.'

'Yeah, I know. But have any more men ridden in apart from the first group of four?'

Billy pondered. 'Another three, less than an hour ago. They split the women and tradesfolk into three buildings, a gunman to each. Mick the saddler's, and the north-side empties that used to be the milliner's and barber's. Me, I ducked down the cellar when they cleared the saloon.'

'Three captors? That only leaves McCabe on the loose.'

Billy nodded brightly. 'The one on the claybank? I think he hitched it somewhere back of the north lots.'

'Yeah. And someplace there could be four bags of booty.'

'Well, maybe you oughta know,' Billy recollected, 'when he was placing his men he said "I'm gonna prepare that marshal's obituary." I thought it was just a sour joke 'cause Fred Venner had seen 'em leave four gunny sacks in the old *CLARION* place. But maybe he was chosing that as his ambush point.'

'Nice thinking, Billy. It tells me where the loot is and confirms where those rifle shots were coming from.'

Billy waggled the shotgun. 'You want I should add support?'

'No. Those scatterguns can pepper innocent folk.' Ben glanced along the fence. 'Mick the saddler's — that's four buildings down?' Noticing Colly watching, he beckoned her forward. 'Billy, you know Colly Wells?' In hushed tones he sketched a plan. 'Can you take her into the saloon? Give me five minutes, then start dickering as though I'm there with you. Raise your voices. An argument could fool McCabe.'

'Where are you gonna be?' Colly whispered anxiously.

'Working my way beyond the saddler's then to the north side. If I can bust McCabe, the others might fold up.'

'Hell, marshal,' Billy objected. 'I ain't no play actor.'

'Colly is, so do your party act.'

'What if McCabe moves?' Colly asked.

'I'm hoping he won't. I want this settled before any hostages end up hurt. And after that, Billy, I'm gonna need you fast.'

'Why? What else you got in mind?'

'You're gonna sell me a long cool drink.'

# SEVENTEEN

As Ben darted along behind the saddler's he heard voices — hostages and captor in muted argument. He paused, peering through Mick's window. Maybe he could use a little help.

A rough-shaven gingery man sat on a half-mended saddle which rested over a stool, nonchalantly fingering his .45. He sounded French-Canadian; Ben guessed him to be one of the two Frank and Colly had seen feeding the team in Sparville. The captives looked subdued. Ben counted three old-timers and the young saddler; and three women, huddled together.

Ben slowly twisted the catch, then kicked the door open with a well-placed foot. The gunnie jumped up, startled.

'Freeze.' In two strides Ben was ramming his iron into the gunnie's belly. The man staggered, winded, dropping his Colt.

'Nice going, marshal.' Mick the saddler gave a welcoming grin of relief. 'Sure glad to see you.'

Ben glanced around; there were more hostages along the back wall. 'Somebody take his gun. Truss him with that rope.'

One of the hostages was Garner, the depot man. While he and Mick were securing the gunslick, Ben said: 'The barman tells me others are being held in the old barber's and milliner's.'

'Marshal,' one bewhiskered oldster began, 'I ain't

meaning to seem ungrateful, but none of us asked for this —'

'Then if you want to help, quit whining.' Ben felt a need to bully them. 'Or if you want to stay safe, keep your heads down while I flush McCabe out. He's in the old *CLARION* house.'

Mick straightened up from tightening the knots. 'You want someone to cover you?'

'Obliged, but it's up to you. This is my fight.'

'That's no reason for refusing help,' said Garner.

Ben inclined his head. 'I'm easily convinced. Those willing to cross the end of the street come with me. But no dead heroes, please.'

Mick found a .44 Remington. Garner took the gunman's Colt. A third volunteer raked up a Navy .36. Ben led them off.

After crossing past the livery to the back of the north side, Ben paused. Now comes the tricky bit, he thought. The printing house stood in isolation beyond the explosives store.

'Ready, Mick?' Ben addressed the other two: 'While I'm tackling McCabe, be thinking how we can handle the two remaining gunmen, though I'm hoping they'll quit once McCabe's out of action. Mick, if McCabe shows his head, keep him pegged down while I make my way in. But no foolish risks.'

And that was the extent of their planning.

The sun was higher now, dropping a hatbrim of shadow across Ben's eyes as he stole forward. He passed some hen coops where chickens pecked aimlessly. Nearer Venner's hut, a pile of dumped boxes formed a convenient screen. As Mick drew alongside, Ben studied the lie of the printing house. Which of the broken windows might McCabe be using? The upper gallery should give a clear view of the south-side doorway where he and Colly had served as targets.

Voices came drifting in – Colly and Billy doing their act. Ben couldn't imagine their pretence of talking with him would fool McCabe for long. He wondered if Colly recalled telling him how she'd wanted to act. Odd, how trivial things stuck in the memory. Maybe it showed how he felt for her.

No time for dallying. McCabe was spitting vengeance with a rifle ... But still no sign of him. The claybank was tied back of the printing house, but the building looked deserted.

'He can't be watching all ways,' Ben muttered. 'I'll take a chance on him facing the street up top. Ain't there a dry ditch starting from here?'

Mick indicated the depression. 'It's mighty shallow cover.'

'Then I'll practice my Indian crawl.'

Leaving Mick by the boxes, Ben slithered along the arroyo. Springing up, he sprinted and flung himself down hard by the printing house wall, grabbing for breath.

He glanced back. The townsmen took no prizes for concealment. The crown of Garner's hat and the rump of his companion were sticking up; but the absence of shots supported McCabe being at the front. Mick was just visible behind the boxes.

Ben peeped through a glassless window frame. The grit-smothered signboard, *BLEAK SPRINGS CLARION*, still lay in gloom amid rusted machinery. Dumped beside it were four bulky sacks – McCabe's booty.

Lifting a leg, Ben pulled himself up on to the sill, cautious of jagged glass. He was poised when the crash of a rifle close by startled him. A backward glance revealed Garner staggering, clutching his shoulder. Mick had dived for the ditch, which left him badly placed. Then Ben saw McCabe.

Hatless, straw hair awry, the ringleader was a mere five yards away at the next window. Intent on shooting, he had still not spotted Ben – just as Ben, concentrating on a silent entry, had failed to notice McCabe.

The gang boss had just jacked a round into the breech for a fresh aim. Ben sensed a frenzy about him, as though his nook of command had become the bolt-hole of a trapped animal.

Ben jumped through the frame, disturbing two chickens squawking amid the ironwork. McCabe whipped round. The rifle swung with him but its barrel bumped against the window jamb.

'Drop it!' Ben snapped.

McCabe complied. In a snarling dive before Ben could aim he yanked out his Colt with the cutaway trigger guard.

There was no sparring space. A large press occupied one wall. A broken table, a smashed filing cabinet in which poultry had nested, took up another. Death was about to close in.

McCabe landed back of an ancient hand press. He shrank behind its frame, Colt roaring. Ben hunkered by a cupboard from which rat-chewed papers had spilled. Slivers of panel ripped at his face. He blasted away as McCabe flitted among the machinery. A symphony of clangs and ricocheting bullets zinged among metalwork. Hens squalled and panicked.

McCabe laughed. 'Lost your touch, marshal?'

Ben eased out a fraction. McCabe had the press frame and a stack of drawers for protection. One drawer stood up-ended. As Ben wormed for position McCabe fired through a gash in its base, sending Ben's gun spinning. Ben crouched defenseless. His foot slipped through a gap in the floorboards, snagging his shin.

McCabe came from around the press, relishing his chance of an accurate shot. Ben reached out, wriggling, and managed to push the cabinet, toppling it towards McCabe. As it hit the press the upper drawers thudded out splintering more rotten boards. Bemused, McCabe set out to stroll round it.

Awkwardly sprawled, Ben struggled to free his leg. McCabe, levelling his Colt, trod on a crumbling board and stumbled, putting the cabinet between them. Ben stretched an arm for his gun. It lay just beyond reach. He groped for something to fling; his hand pushed against matted straw. He felt something smooth and curved. An egg. He hurled it. It smashed into McCabe's face, releasing a stench that betrayed its age.

McCabe looked astonished, insulted even. As he wiped yolk from his eyes, Ben jerked his foot free and seized his Colt.

McCabe blundered forward, shooting blindly down. Ben twisted up his gun and fired.

Pain. It lanced through Ben as powder-burn stung his jaw and earlobe. Gunsmoke raked his nostrils, swamping the stink of the egg. He detached himself from the dying weight of McCabe and knelt against the press, suddenly aware of how his limbs were shaking. It took him some moments to grasp that McCabe's last bullet had veered past him. The scorching was too real.

Presently he subsided. He got to his feet, still swaying a little, dabbing the blood on his chin. The shot which had knocked his Colt loose had added raw flesh to his hand. Reaching the window, he leant on the sill. Mick was closer now, but hesitating.

'You in good shape, marshal?' Mick called. When Ben acknowledged, he said: 'Those other two gunhawks seem about to cry quits. They've been shouting to each other.'

'Then I got a message for 'em.' As Ben saw Colly approaching he sucked in a lungful and hollered:

'This is Marshal Ben Galliard. Now listen good. McCabe's dead. So are three others. Those holding prisoners take note. You're outnumbered. Hand over your guns. Give yourselves up.'

# EIGHTEEN

Outside the printing house Colly presented Ben with the longest embrace he'd experienced in some while. While Colly saw to the horses, Ben jailed the last of the gunmen then had the four sacks of booty transferred into the security of Venner's hut. Then he sat down to wait outside the surgery while Pinebox Keel dealt with the bodies. Doc Mason rode up.

'Thought I heard shooting. How long you been waiting?'

Ben managed a wry smile. 'Long enough.' He felt a comic sense of relief when Mason planted himself alongside and began to scrutinize him. 'You'll have one or two other customers. Garner stopped a slug but it ain't serious.'

'Let's start with you.' Mason rummaged in his bag for bandage. 'You oughta duck lower. What happened to your ear?'

'Powder-burn mainly. Kinda tender though.'

While Mason applied salve, Ben described the gunfight. Doc chuckled. 'First time I've heard of a gunslinger being cold-cocked by an egg. Must remember that. So – what next?'

'I'm aiming to quit marshalling. Now don't look disappointed, Doc. I only took it on because I owed it to Charlie Priest. And I'm only sorry McCabe came gunning for me in Bleak. But I made a bad start in Sparville with Sheriff Quayle. We weren't in tune.'

'Over the bank raid? ... Exceptional circumstances.'

'Maybe so, but ...' Ben crinkled his eyes towards the western hills. 'Sparville and Bleak ain't that far apart. It's important their peace officers get on.'

Mason sighed. 'Yeah, well ...' He closed his bag. 'There'll be a visiting judge through soon to deal with the three you've jailed. And the booty'll have to go back to Sparville. I suppose you'll be returning to cow work?'

Ben nodded. 'But on the home ranch. With brother Frank, I hope.' He rose as Colly approached. 'You got the horses settled?'

'Sure. Jimmy's getting a livery full of gunmen's nags.' She studied Ben's ointmented features with curiosity. 'Ben, I never got you asked. How did you get that face?'

'Simple. By rolling around in rotten eggs.'

'What? ... You're crazy.'

Davison approached his store. Ben called to him: 'I'll be in to seek another new shirt. Hope you've plenty in stock.'

'Marshal, I'll give you a new shirt free. You deserve it.'

As Ben grinned his thanks he saw Jensen clopping up.

'I've been hearing some alarming tales,' the Rocking Y boss said. 'You're lucky you're in one piece, Ben.'

'Wa-all, maybe. Let's hope your working season stays trouble-free.'

'The rustling ain't as bad as we thought. I've patched up differences with the Cut Circle, and we don't reckon our other neighbours were involved ... You wouldn't consider coming back, Ben? Tophand, extra pay.'

Ben shook his head slowly. 'No thanks, Mr

Jensen. Nor am I staying on here.' He unclipped his badge and handed it to Doc. 'Mostly I brought trouble to Bleak Springs.' Mason took the star and exchanged resigned glances with Jensen.

Ben said: 'This town ain't big enough for a marshal. All you need is a jailhouse janitor. Maybe you could send that badge on to Joe — the wagoner's lad in Sparville. He gave me some help. I think he'd like it for a souvenir.'

Billy hollered from over the batwings. 'Marshal! you still needing that long cool drink?'

Ben licked his lips, testing for dryness, and sought Colly's eye for approval. 'Maybe we'll both look in later if the lady don't object.' She rewarded him with a smile.

'I'll have a schooner sitting on the bar for you,' Billy promised. 'But make it soon. Coupla days, I could be low on beer.'

'Coupla days, we could be riding out. We'll visit your folks, Colly, then call back here to see if Frank's showed. Then we'll aim south ... But, Billy — pledge me one thing. Don't let any gunslingers shoot chips off that mirror. It's one of the finest I've seen.'

Billy grinned with pleasure. 'You mean that?'

'Sure. And whenever I come riding through Bleak Springs I'll expect to find it in one piece.'

Three mornings later, Ben and Colly were an hour's ride west, roan and mare holding a handsome pace. They rode contentedly, until Colly emerged from her thoughts.

'Fancy you remembering I liked play-acting.'

'Yeah. It only shows, first impressions can be lasting.'

An approaching horseman hallooed them. It was Frank. They drew rein until he cantered up. Ben voiced a trace of doubt to Colly. 'I hope you two are still gonna see eye to eye.'

'Howdy both,' Frank opened. 'The lady smiles, but I guess I heard that last remark. Must be the morning breeze.'

'Must be.' Ben grinned. 'How's the leg mending?'

'I'm forking a horse, ain't I?' Frank glanced at Colly. 'To help make amends I brought you a message from Quayle. I weren't sure we'd meet up, but it's to say your Grandpa's gold's still safe and it's there when you need it.'

'Thank you, Frank. I'm beholden to you.'

Frank leant on the pommel, his eyes crinkling towards Ben. 'And back at Buffalo Skulls I spoke to a coupla riders just out from Bleak.'

'So you've heard about McCabe?' Ben tilted his head. 'The shooting's over, Frank. So's the marshalling. Account settled.'

'But ain't you due for a reward? For Cricklewood?'

'Am I? If I am, I'll put it into the ranch.'

'Ben might take up chicken farming,' Colly teased, her eyes twinkling. 'He's found a new use for rotten eggs.'

'He's what?' Mystified, Frank pushed back his hat. 'I thought he was dragging me home to run the place.'

'We'll tell you as we go. But I'm sure taking Colly.'

'Like that, is it?'

'Like that. You've made up your mind – to run the place?'

'I ain't making no promises.' Frank glanced slyly from Ben to Colly. 'Looks like the promising's already been made.'

'Ignore him,' Ben grinned. 'Frank, there's one sure promise – she's gonna take to Ma's home cooking.'

Masking her blushes, Colly smiled. 'Wait till your Ma's had a taste of mine.'

Ben flicked the reins. Swinging the roan he set pace for the southern range.